T0161389

WALASCHEK'S
DREAM

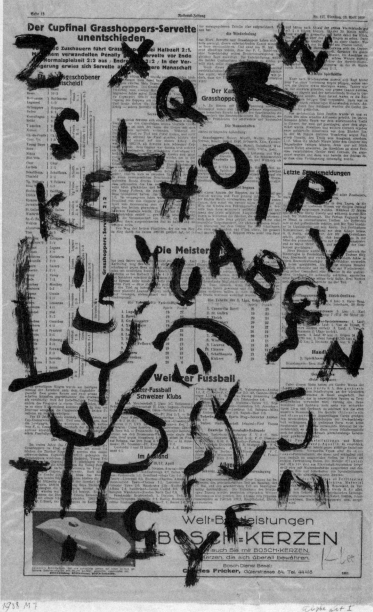

GIOVANNI ORELLI

WALASCHEK'S
DREAM

Translated by Jamie Richards
Introduction by Daniel Rothenbühler

DALKEY ARCHIVE PRESS
CHAMPAIGN • DUBLIN • LONDON

Originally published in Italian as *Il sogno di Walacek* by Giulio Einaudi Editore S.p.A., 1991
Copyright © 1991 by Giovanni Orelli
Translation and notes copyright © 2012 by Jamie Richards
Introduction © 2012 by Daniel Rothenbühler
Introduction translation © 2012 by Aaron Kerner
First edition, 2012

Frontispiece: Paul Klee
Alphabet I, 1938, 187
colored paste on paper on cardboard
53,9 x 34,4 cm
Zentrum Paul Klee, Bern

Library of Congress Cataloging-in-Publication Data

Orelli, Giovanni, 1928-
[Sogno di Walacek. English]
Walaschek's dream / Giovanni Orelli ; translated by Jamie Richards. -- 1st ed.
    p. cm.
"Originally published in Italian as Il sogno di Walacek by Giulio Einaudi Editore S.p.A., 1991."
ISBN 978-1-56478-756-9 (pbk. : alk. paper) -- ISBN 978-1-56478-722-4 (cloth : alk. paper)
I. Richards, Jamie. II. Title.
PQ4875.R4S6513 2012
853'.914--dc23
                    2012002891

Partially funded by a grant from the Illinois Arts Council, a state agency

The publication of this work was supported by a grant from Pro Helvetia, Swiss Arts Council

 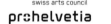 

www.dalkeyarchive.com

Cover: design and composition by Sarah French
Printed on permanent/durable acid-free paper and bound in the United States of America

CONTENTS

INTRODUCTION

A Dream-Dance on the Brink

When asked which of his twenty books—novels, stories, poems, essays—is his favorite, Giovanni Orelli always replies: "*Walaschek's Dream*." It's the book he enjoyed writing most; in truth, he'd written it more for himself than for others. Even now he precisely remembers the day that the idea for the book occurred to him. As a participant in a plenary session of the Swiss UNESCO commission, he'd been invited to visit the Klee exhibition at the Bern Museum of Fine Arts. In a neighboring room he'd stumbled upon the painting *Alphabet I*, which Klee had composed on a page of the *National Zeitung* from April 19, 1938—a sports page with a description of the Swiss Cup final match between Zürich's FC Grasshoppers and Geneva's FC Servette. Immediately he felt the desire to write a book based on this picture. And in doing so, to let himself be governed only by his fancies, his mental associations, his dreams, without a thought for the work's eventual reader, its eventual readability, its ultimate significance. He'd known that *something* would emerge, but couldn't have said what. He was in the same position as the painter in Cervantes's *Don*

Quixote, who, when asked what he was painting, replied: "Whatever comes out."

Thus, not only is a significant part of the book concerned with an actual game of soccer, it resembles one too, in its haphazardness, its unpredictability. Yet at the very beginning of the novel, Orelli gives a hint as to what will lend the whole thing, in spite of this contingency, a specific trajectory. He records: "This work was written on the occasion of the 700th anniversary of the Swiss Confederation, with the support of Pro Helvetia." In 1991, when the novel appeared, this simple comment carried a tremendous, even an explosive force. For that 700-year anniversary celebration would be boycotted by the lion's share of Switzerland's creative artists—most of Orelli's writer colleagues, male and female, among them. In November 1989, as the Berlin Wall came down, it had been revealed that the Swiss state security apparatus had spied and opened dossiers on more than 700,000 persons—including almost all of the country's artists—during the course of the Cold War. For the creative community, the celebration's boycott was a settling of accounts with the entire Cold War era.

A Critical Panorama of Switzerland

But in *Walaschek's Dream*, Orelli settled accounts with Switzerland's history in an altogether different manner. By beginning with Klee's *Alphabet I*—and Walaschek, the footballer who emerges from it—and playfully unfolding a whole web of facts and fictions, Orelli was able to circumvent both boycott and celebration, revealing the contradictions of a Switzerland as cosmopolitan as it was parochial, as magnanimous as it was petty, founded as much on freedom as on constraint. In contrast with Frisch and Dürrenmatt, Orelli was as willing to stress his country's good points as he was to criticize. Dürrenmatt, in his speech in honor of Václav Havel in November, 1990, likened Switzerland to a prison. In response, Orelli pointed out what Noam Chomsky had said about the USA, the frequent target of the latter's criticism: That in spite of all, they'd never harmed a single hair on his head.

Like Chomsky, Orelli in *Walaschek's Dream*, addressing Switzerland, uses precisely this freedom to mercilessly reveal, for instance, how reluctant his country was to absorb those pursued by the neighboring Nazi regime. He repeatedly cites Marc Vuilleumier's 1987 study, *Immigrants and Refugees in Switzerland*, in order to demonstrate how the Swiss authorities, as early as 1933, sought to make Switzerland "a transit country rather than a land of asylum," striving "to prevent the refugees from remaining by urging them on with strict sanctions, or even physically deporting them. The threats, boycotts, and acts of violence to which Jews as such were exposed weren't sufficient for them to be considered political refugees." And in 1938—the year Klee's *Alphabet I* was painted—the Swiss implemented new entry requirements for Austrians in the wake of the annexation of that country to the greater German Reich, while at the same time smoothly granting business partners the same visas they denied the refugees. To characterize these policies of the Swiss in dealing with Jewish refugees, Orelli borrows the withering verdict of Sigmund Freud: "Switzerland is not one of the hospitable countries." Thus, in its apparently playful wealth of associations, *Walaschek's Dream* does indeed proffer a highly critical panorama of Switzerland and Europe in the era of Walaschek's stardom and the creation of Klee's *Alphabet I*—a panorama that retained its relevance during the political dust-ups of 1991, and continues to do so today. Yet Walaschek and Klee interest Orelli not merely because the former, a stateless half-Russian, had to be accepted as Swiss by the World Soccer Association before the Swiss authorities would do the same, and because the latter, though born in Switzerland, and granted asylum in 1933, was denied naturalization in 1934 due to a May 1933 treaty with Nazi Germany.

Deliver Me From the Limbo of Oblivion
In both Klee and Walaschek, Orelli demonstrates how leading national figures emerge and endure—or fail to do so. For in 1991, the national heroes of the 700-year-old Switzerland were no longer William Tell and Arnold Winkelried—mythical figures—but rather athletes, artists, writers, and scientists. Yet the athlete Walaschek and the artist Klee were perceived quite differently: in 1938 Walaschek was the man of the hour, but today is in danger of being completely forgotten; in his own time Klee was barely known, but for our own generation, and those to come, his worth is uncontested. As Orelli writes, "The artist is generally a fire that burns slowly and can singe anyone who comes near for centuries. Not so the soccer player—he has to do whatever he can in a hurry, burning with a bright but short-lived flame, like the bonfires on Swiss National Day, August 1st, made with tree branches and dry twigs—fleeting."

Walaschek the footballer would have vanished from our consciousness today if not for Klee's *Alphabet I*, in which his name is half-obliterated—and thus emphasized—by the O from Klee's alphabet, whose letters are scattered wildly across the sheet of newsprint; and if not for Scribe O/17360, "orelligiovanni," who investigates this O and half-obliterated name, as well as registry number 1736 in the crematorium at Lugano, and the life and work that lie behind it: those of Paul Klee. This is the core of Walaschek's dream: that his temporary fame as a footballer will be eternalized, that he will persist in the minds of men. "So the dream was: would there be someone for me, will there? Please come! Oh Berkeley of the *esse est percipi*, deliver me from the limbo of oblivion. From the gray weight that keeps me down in this pit." Because, "like a trail of snail slime," sport leaves behind only "a few statistics, trophies, press reports like the one in the April 19th *National Zeitung*: a trivial heap of petty talk. It's the herbarium, the museum of the banal, it's death. Klee wanted to paint death."

Thus, one of the central themes of *Walaschek's Dream* is the fundamental need—not just Walaschek's, but everyone's—not to disappear completely after death. According to the empiricist idealism of George Berkeley (1685–1753), however, only what is perceived can be said to exist: *esse est percipi*. So Walaschek must leave behind permanent traces, not merely the ephemeral trail— the "snail slime"—of statistics, trophies, or press reports. And Klee provided just such permanent traces. By means of the artist's *Alphabet I*, and the text founded upon it by Scribe O/17360, Walaschek will be immortalized. Yet Orelli's text doesn't follow Berkeley quite so far as to suggest that Walaschek continues to exist *only* because he remains perceptible through Klee's painting and the work of Scribe O/17360. To the idealist Berkeley, Orelli opposes the materialist Bertrand Russell, for whom the sensory data available to human perception signals the actual existence of things, even if these things are themselves situated in a space beyond our ken.

The World as Will and Idea

Orelli brings both Berkeley and Russell into play by means of facetious, ironic quotations, which mutually relativize each other. More serious are his references to Arthur Schopenhauer, who is taken up and pursued again and again over the course of the text. In fact, Schopenhauer's philosophy in *The World as Will and Idea* allows the book to unite even Berkeley and Russell. Schopenhauer's concept of the blind Will—continually driving onward toward existence, commanding all and binding all together—resembles Kant's "thing-in-itself" insofar as it is veiled from direct human sensory perception, yet differs in being tangible as the common mainspring of every action of men and beasts. So that human perceptions of space, time, and causality are available, but not until the individuated appearance of the Will obtains subjective validity. We recognize the world in Schopenhauer as we do in Berkeley—that is, only insofar as we perceive it subjectively; yet, as in Russell, this representation is not exhaustive, but rather implies a force situated beyond space, time, and causality.

Even if these conceptual conjunctions materialize in the text as if through free association, and are always ironically undercut, they are by no means mere intellectual gimmickry. That is to say, the text localizes the Schopenhauerian Will both in Walaschek's dream—his unconditional drive to secure a continued existence for himself beyond his football career and his lifetime—as well as in the realization of that dream through Klee's *Alphabet I* and the text of Scribe O/17360. For how did Walaschek and Klee cross paths with each other in the first place? They knew nothing about one another—were, as the text says, "two 'constellations' that hadn't met." It's unlikely that Klee took any notice of the description of the football game, or even the name Walaschek: "he was only aware of having in front of him a page from the newspaper concerning sports." The momentous branding of Walaschek's name with Klee's O occurred purely by chance. That accident, however, leads the text back to Schopenhauer's blindly surging Will: "there the erasure of half the name is the product of *Wille*." And blind Will lies behind the free associations of Scribe O/17360 as well: drawing, as Klee does, on wildly diverse materials, Orelli assembles them into complex collages, astonishing juxtapositions. Here blind Will gives rise—as in Darwin's account of natural selection—to an abundance of unforeseen meanings, which either flourish in conjunction or founder again, so that what finally emerges is a finely nuanced and supremely organized whole. Orelli treats this seemingly Darwinian collaboration of accident and order with an almost mocking irony, for example, by using an excerpt from *Abandonment to Divine Providence*, by the French Jesuit Jean-Pierre de Caussade, to describe a successful center-shot in terms of the paradoxes of quietist devotion. But that description, in turn, is perfectly suited to the style of writing employed in *Walaschek's Dream*: "Without method, yet most exact; without rule, yet most orderly; without reflection, yet most profound; without skill, yet thoroughly well-constructed, without effort, yet accomplishing everything; and without foresight, yet nothing could be better suited to unexpected events."

The Greatest Fortune that Can Befall an Author

How readers should approach this unmethodically exact, irregularly ordered, unreflectively profound, and unexpectedly harmonious whole, the text leaves entirely to them. In a fictional dialogue set in an inn (which evokes a learned dispute of the Middle Ages) an innumerable succession of interpretive hypotheses—now contradicting each other, now confirming each other—are tabled in an attempt to get to the bottom of the riddle of the O branding Walaschek's name. This sprawling allegorization points to the difficulty of any interpretation that attempts to extract a particular message from a single pictorial element, like Klee's O: "Interpreting an O is like interpreting a note on a trumpet, a solitary note that breaks through a pastoral solitude, in a trumpet concerto or Christmas oratorio, spurted out by a *tuba mirum spargens sonum per deserta regionum*, by a Stravinsky; and a furious hand turns off the radio, and there it lingers, in the dark, that single note, all night long."

The interpretation of the O is all the more futile in that Klee applied his alphabet to the sports page "with swift hand, the hand of a divine thief . . . a few hieroglyphics with the appearance of masks: signs of a 'language no longer known?' The song of the birds, the flight of the sparrows, the language of the Spanish gypsies?" These signs are—in Schopenhauer's terms—part of the representation, which remains individual, subjective, and does not allow us to recognize the world itself—the Will—in which it has its source. But as part of a work of art, they do let us understand, as it were, nature's "half-spoken words," (Schopenhauer) even if we're unable to translate this understanding into conceptual knowledge. Hence, with Schopenhauerian sympathy, Klee lays his arm on the shoulder of Scribe O/17360, and consoles him: "My friend, don't wear yourself out. You don't have to explain my O. The greatest fortune that can befall an author is not to be read, a painter not to be seen, or to be seen with haste, like on those horrendous group museum tours: as long as the work is talked about, obviously. Or, if they see you, if they read you, you're fortunate to be misunderstood. If they understand you, no one will think you're right; if they don't understand you, everyone will project onto you their inchoate desires, their secret dreams. And your success is assured. You have to be mysterious, like a witch or an astrologist, people have always had a need for magicians and sorcerers." The plethora of interpretations of the O presented in *Walaschek's Dream* is, above all, an invitation to the readers of this book to give their "inchoate desires" and "secret dreams" free rein, to let themselves free-associate, to form their own images of Switzerland, Walaschek, and Klee.

Classical Poetry and Modern Sport
And in those images, as in Orelli's text, the most heterogeneous elements will come together: the pyramidal structure of the Swiss Cup and the conceptual pyramids of Aristotle; the Greater German team in the 1938 match against Switzerland and Wagner's *Lohengrin*; the 4-2 victory of the Swiss team in that match and the great nineteenth-century writer Gottfried Keller; Walaschek's disappearance into the archives of FC Servette and the eighteenth-century empiricist idealist George Berkeley. The text pushes its game of combining tremendously disparate fields especially far in the series of team lineups that appear to Walaschek in his dream,

lineups that set sundry historical figures cheek-by-jowl with the greats of football:

Pulver

Alcibiades Hannibal

Lempen Socrates Aristotle

Plotinus Walaschek Plato Vonlanthen Sulla

When somebody in the text asks why the Roman dictator Sulla deserves to be included, the reason given is the mellifluousness of his name: "It's a nice name, fast, for a winger." These lineups are based on the laws of poetry, like the catalog of ships in Homer's *Iliad*: the names of the Portuguese team facing off against the Swiss on May 1, 1938, roar from "a loudspeaker made of fascist alloy" in Milan like the prelude to a madrigal, in decasyllabic and enneasyllabic lines:

Azevédo   Simóes   Gustávo

Amáro   Albíno   Pereíra

Likewise, the names of Italy's three fullbacks yield—according to Italian metrics—eleven syllables, with accents on the fourth, eighth, and tenth:

Bacigalúpo

Ballarín   Maróso

binding them smoothly to verses by Dante, Ariosto, and Saba:

mi ritrovaí   per una sélva   oscúra

e per la sélva	*a tutta bríglia*	*il cáccia*
mi stringerá	*per un pensiéro*	*il cuóre*
Bacigalúpo	Ballarín	Maróso

This blending of classical poetry and modern sport has more than merely the comic appeal of burlesque, which transforms the sublime into the banal, the banal into the sublime. It is the manifestation of an artistic and literary vision with the power to effect the playful levitation of the extremes of dualistic thought—not merely the sublime and banal, but big and little, true and false, intention and accident. So that the joking can suddenly turn bitterly earnest, as for instance at Klee's death, when the following lineup is given:

†

† †

† † †

† † † † †

and for the opposing team, the mouths of cannons at the ready:

o o o o o

o o o

o o

o

Walaschek's Dream is a dream-dance on the brink: for all its playfulness, the book maintains its gravity, evoking the tremendous suffering of the era of 1938, and of those individuals who failed to survive it—for instance, the Austrian footballer Matthias Sindelar, the "Mozart of soccer," a Jew who was found dead under mysterious circumstances following the *Anschluss* of Austria to Greater Germany in January, 1939.

An Enduring Tension

Alongside the many historical figures, Orelli brings forward a series of fictional characters, most notably the daughter of Walaschek's coach in Geneva, and in Ticino one Giulia Sismondi, who befriends the crematorium employee Cesare Rossi and carries Klee's ashes to his widow—a scene full of restrained poetry. Throughout the text, what captivates the reader is a parallelism and intertwining of caustic irony and pressing solemnity, sober precision and fantastical creativity, disturbing grotesquery and bewitching poetry. Which is why the book never allows itself to be pinned down to any particular genre: Is it a novel? An essay? A *capriccio*? A treatise? It has something of all of these, and in its density and plenitude fuses the cosmopolitan urbanity of a big-city novel with the alehouse tableaus of a village tale.

This tension between transgressive expansion and retreat into a manageable smallness reflects the career of the author, who hails from a tiny village in the high-lying Bedretto Valley, near the Saint-Gotthard Massif, and was trained as a philologist and historian in the Northern Italian metropolis of Milan. Orelli feels far more at home in both of these places—high-altitude village and bustling conurbation—than in the little city of Lugano, where for years now he's taught in a high school and worked as a literary critic.

This fusion of cosmopolitanism and provincialism is on display in Orelli's manifold work as a translator. Along with the Latin classics, he has translated Emily Dickinson and Dylan Thomas into his native dialect, that of the Bedretto Valley, rather than into standard Italian—not out of verbal conservatism, but a delight in experimentation, and because certain basic motives for human existence are better preserved in dialect's archaisms and turns of phrase than in orthodox speech. Thus, in *Walaschek's Dream*, the reader will rediscover numerous dialect expressions, the traces of an individuated manifestation of the Will—an enduring tension that, in its translation to a world language, will certainly not be lost.

DANIEL ROTHENBÜHLER, 2012
TRANSLATED BY AARON KERNER

AUTHOR'S NOTE

Genia Walaschek's biography comes directly from the forward of the 1940s Swiss national soccer team himself. I thank him, as well as another national player, Franco Andreoli, for the information they shared with me, and especially Sergio Grandini for providing me with the documents regarding Klee's death. This work was written on the occasion of the 700th anniversary of the Swiss Confederation, with the support of Pro Helvetia. It's almost superfluous to add that there are numerous invented characters (such as the coach's daughter, Silvia of Silenen, Giulia Sismondi, etc.) living (or trying to live) alongside the "historical" figures (from Walaschek to Klee, from Schopenhauer to . . .) mentioned in this book.

WALASCHEK'S
DREAM

But Pardon, gentles all,
The flat unraisèd spirits that hath dared
On this unworthy scaffold to bring forth
So great an object. Can this cockpit hold
The vasty fields of France? Or may we cram
Within this wooden O the very casques
That did affright the air at Agincourt?
O pardon: since a crookèd figure may
Attest in little place a million,
And let us, ciphers to this great account,
On your imaginary forces work.

Shakespeare, Henry V

Attendi attendi,
Magnanimo campion (s'alla veloce
Piena degli anni il tuo valor contrasti
La spoglia di tuo nome), attendi e il core
Movi ad alto desio.

Giacomo Leopardi, "A un vincitore nel pallone"

The 1938 Swiss Cup final took place on April 18 in Bern. At the time, the unwritten rule was that the final had to be played on Easter Monday, and always in the capital of the Confederation. Christ was still risen on April 17, 1938, and so hearts could open (as they say) to hope, even if on that April 16 (Holy Saturday!) the newspaper reported that in the last three weeks, there had been 140 suicides in Vienna.

Naturally, not everybody chose suicide. Many people led (as they say) normal lives, or nearly. Others lived on in the prisons. A correspondent from the *News Chronicle* reported that 12,000 people were still imprisoned in Vienna alone, and 40,000 others in the various provinces of the former Austrian state. That is, more than could fit in Bern's Wankdorf Stadium, where the National Cup final was held.

This digression on Vienna isn't due to the fact that Vienna, unlike London, had made itself a virtual Academy of Soccer, as the cradle, the roost, the home of the famous Wunderteam, that sublime model of classical soccer, which the provincials (and that includes the Swiss) couldn't take their eyes off of. Vienna was finished being capital of the Hapsburg Empire, home of the imperial eagle. Austria was finished, an appetizer for Adolf Hitler's Germany. And the great Matthias Sindelar, star of the Wunderteam, was finished too.

Before going back to the final in Bern, one last note about Vienna. The prisoners there were diplomats, members of the aristocracy, or Jews. And yet, with nary a trace of irony, a "Letter from Vienna" dated April 29, published as an "editorial" in a respected Italian-Swiss newspaper, the *Corriere del Ticino*, ended by saying: "Nationalism gives the Austrians *panem et circenses*. Isn't that enough to ensure their welfare and inspire a sense of boundless gratitude for their liberator?"

Yes, before returning to the green oasis that is the Wankdorf, we mustn't fail to mention that, at least for those who weren't yet born in 1938, on April 10, Palm Sunday, there was a plebiscite (called by Hitler) in Germany and Austria (excluding, of course, the Israelites) on the *Anschluss* to ratify public approval of Germany's annexation of Austria, which had taken place that March. In the German Reich, out of 99.452% of all voters, 99.06% voted yes, and 0.94% no. In Austria, out of 53,996 voters of the ex-army, 53,872 said yes, 76 no. Hitler, the papers reported, was "satisfied." On April 3, General Zehner, ex-head of the ex-Austrian army, killed himself.

On April 18, the day of the Swiss Cup final in Bern, there was a strong wind, but the field was in excellent shape. Is it wind that ruffles flags, or is it flags that, like women's skirts, stir up the wind?

1938 seems like a golden year for flags. Even on February 6 in Cologne (Köln), at the Germany-Switzerland game (soccer, of course! final score 1-1), "countless" Nazi flags "fluttered in the sun." For Hitler's visit to his great friend, Italy, planned for that spring in Rome, "the pillars on Via Nazionale were to bear sheaves (*fasces*) of flags, as would the tall pedestals on Via dell'Impero." Flags everywhere, to accompany the notes of *Lohengrin*, Act Two:

> *Der Rache Werk sei nun beschworen*
> *aus meines Busens wilder Nacht!*
>
> (May the work of revenge be conjured up
> from the wild night of my breast!)

Yes, the twentieth century is a century of flags. Later, long after 1938, a Russian said, "I think that the country would do a hell of a lot better if it had for its national banner not that foul double-headed imperial fowl or the vaguely masonic hammer-and-sickle, but the flag of the Russian Navy: our glorious, incomparably beautiful flag of St. Andrew: the diagonal blue cross against a virgin-white background."

Switzerland, too, came to learn the importance of flags. Studying *dividual and individual structural elements*, the painter Paul Klee carefully examines the Swiss cross. He says: "I shall show you some cases, in which the problem is posed both concisely and cogently," and then observes: "The individual pattern, called a cross, now agrees quite well with the structural aspect. The two mesh. Is this indeed an individual pattern? Yes, an individual pattern of the character of a regular cross. Structure has been shifted into a cross."

Even back in 1914, during a speech in Zurich on December 14 (remember that, unfortunately, World War I, as they call it, had broken out a few months earlier), Swiss writer Carl Spitteler—who would go on to win the Nobel Prize in literature—astutely noted that we Swiss "have in common neither blood, language, nor a ruling dynasty that could attenuate our contrasts and unite us on a higher level; we don't even have a real capital. These are elements of political weakness, let's not fool ourselves. We need a symbol that can help us overcome, help us transcend these elements of weakness. Fortunately, we have such a symbol. I don't need to tell you: it's the flag of the Confederation." On a higher level: honor to Carl Spitteler.

On the highest pole at Wankdorf, one flag would wave above the flags of Geneva and Zurich: the national flag.

One year earlier—that is, in 1913, and this time in Zurich's rival city (in terms of sports, economics, *esprit*), Geneva, home of Calvin and Rousseau, another bard, a member of a minority within a minority—in other words, a writer from Italian Switzerland—Francesco Chiesa, was asked to share his thoughts on that complicated mosaic that is our little land, speaking there in Helvetia's main "Roman" city. He didn't discuss the 3,000 plus pieces of that mosaic, our inherent resistance to everything that comes from the capital, or the conservatism in our blood. Instead he spoke—to great applause—about the camaraderie among the confederate peoples as a model for Europe and for the world. He ended with an analogy destined for posterity: the confederate peoples of Switzerland are like the columns of a Greek temple: "they all lean slightly, each imperceptibly tilting toward a single axis, in such a way that, seen alone, they seem straight on their bases, free in their bearing, just and perfect in their individuality; seen together, they appear—as they are—of one mind, in harmony. The eye doesn't notice how those marble lines slant; yet following them upward, it unconsciously rises to the ideal vertex where the entire temple converges . . . The Greek temple is a pyramid whose tip we cannot see."

How high up is the tip? That ideal vertex? How far above the clouds? Up there with the astronauts? Next to God? Some Catholic newspapers, in fact, criticized Chiesa for sounding Platonic, not Christian. *Tu platonicus es, non christianus.*

The Swiss Cup is more Aristotelian than Platonic. And the single-elimination tournament, which ended the day after Christ's resurrection (in the capital, even if Bern—as Carl Spitteler rightly points out—is no Vienna, London, Paris, Madrid, or Rome), forms a perfect pyramid.

At the base of the pyramid are all the soccer teams in the country, starting with the fourth division. *Id est,* not all three thousand of the country's municipalities participate in the tournament. Some alpine villages would have to include the priest and the priest's housekeeper to make an eleven-person team. They don't have anything even resembling a football pitch. Maybe a patch for planting potatoes, as when the great Traugott Wahlen's great plan was implemented, in the years when the country was completely surrounded by the Axis powers. But real soccer is something else entirely. For example, a town like Ossasco, in the High Ticino, on the south side of the National Redoubt (or in peacetime, the St. Gotthard Massif), is a miniscule community. It could only matter in the mind of a linguist studying such miniscule archaeologies, due to the fact that its name ends in –*asco*, which indicates Ligurian provenance. Ossasco would have to mobilize everyone aged sixty to ninety, borrowing players from the surrounding areas, including the priest, and import a half team or so of Brazilians to make up its eleven-man "Dinamo Ossasco":

Eliseo

Djalma Santos   Nilton Santos

Franku 't Zan   Santisteban   Gervàs

Manuel   Attilio   Ademir   Vincenzo   Rico

– With Eliseo at the goal? Isn't he over seventy?

Scribe O/17360 shrugged—what else could he do? When someone asked whether people in Ossasco got married anymore, they'd reply: – Bah . . . who knows? Maybe Eliseo, one day, one day—*a passàn lè* . . .

Eliseo, on his bench in the corner, was silent. If someone had actually asked him to play goalie for Dinamo Ossasco, if that was what General Guisan wanted, he would have said, Yes sir! Just like during Carnival, when everyone dressed in costumes and told him, Play us a polka! he played a polka. The harmonica would practically disappear into his Nietzsche-esque mustache. He played quite badly, but tears still welled up in his eyes because polkas reminded him of the young lady who would eventually become his wife, Emilia del Carlone, since passed on, who'd lived just long enough to see the "frin-fron" (gramophone) in Ossasco, and for weeks on end had talked of nothing but the gramophone and what wonders man was capable of inventing. What did they invent in Germany, which was on the cutting edge of technology, on April 18, 1938? Emilia del Carlone had no idea—she didn't even know the word "technology." But the new gramophone at the Osteria dell'Angelo gave her an idea.

So there's no Dinamo Ossasco; Eliseo can keep on drinking his drink in peace. Only teams properly registered with the ASF, the Swiss Football Association, can play. It's extremely rare for a minor team to reach the quarterfinals, though not out of the question. So, starting with the thirty-second (final), the newspapers report on the pyramid as it rises.

In the same issue as an account of the speech given by Seyss-Inquart, Austrian Minister of the Interior, who proclaimed Austria's freedom in Linz (on March 6), and a transcript of the speech by Cardinal Innitzer, Archbishop of Vienna, appealing to Austrian Catholics (two days before the Ides of March), telling them to thank God for having enabled the great political changes in Austria to take place without bloodshed and to pray for a happy future for everyone ("All orders from the authorities must be willingly obeyed"), our local papers highlighted the endeavors (*exploits*) of the small district and village teams: Tramelan, Nidau, Sementina. A team of immigrants (the Dopolavoro: when they win they dedicate their victory to the Duce's portrait in the hall of the Casa d'Italia; when they lose they seem to ask his clemency) would be completely content just to go up against the "titled" Servette (losing 3-0), just as a peasant would be happy for the rest of his days if he made it onto his party's electoral list: there in alphabetical order, on the same level as a lawyer or entrepreneur . . . But who would, naturally, get clobbered by the competition—that is, in the words of the municipal clerk, who always carries a club (you never know)—*clobbered* like Dopolavoro by Servette—but that's democracy!

Once in a while, one of these minor teams miraculously manages to reach the top of the pyramid, which narrows more and more as the months pass. Mezzovico vs. Zurich! Until atop the summit of that Matterhorn risen from the process of fair elimination but a single flag will wave. Between March and April, tension mounts—people are, of course, placing their bets—until there are two semi-finalists who will face off on April 18 at the Wankdorf in Bern.

When a minor team beats a titled team, public sentiment is divided between joy and sadness. Sadness due to the elimination of the favorite; but then, for some, a secret joy in seeing that, every so often—or every death of a pope, as we say (and some would say that popes never—or almost never—die)—David comes back and beats Goliath. The Davids of History: David himself, Finland, Sementina . . . And the Goliaths? In Finland's case, there's Russia—i.e., the devil. And as for Sementina? Sementina is each and every one of us, from the first day of the work week to the last. In theory, even a peaceful Acquistapace, a prayerful Diotallevi, a hopeful Sperandio, *oriundi* from Brianza, or other recent arrivals to the motherland from an even more southerly parallel, naturalized in the '20s, say in Pedrinate (the southernmost village in Switzerland), could theoretically be elected federal councilor, become

President of the Confederation, reach the top of the nation, in the same way that a black man could also aspire, theoretically, to be world champion, like a Joe Louis who can show a Max Schmeling what's what. A black man could even aspire, theoretically, to be President of the United States, Othello to be the Doge.

And Julius Caesar knew very well that the life of a mountain village rests on a fierce battle for survival.

In 1938 there were two teams, two big families with two silly names, that kept rising to the top: the Grasshoppers, from Zurich, and Servette (maids), the name of a district in Geneva. These are the two teams that supplied the raw material for the National team: six Grasshoppers, and four from Servette. The eleventh spot was filled from Lugano, a team that had reached the semi-finals, thus representing the "third" Switzerland, that of the Italic ethnicity, who—thanks to their whimsy and imagination—are always useful, especially in the penalty area (did Amadò leave Lugano for the Grasshoppers because the Grasshoppers, reportedly backed by the local Jews, offered him a substantial, well-deserved reward, the best position, with help from Firestone?). Thus, our football is a perfect antonomasia for the harmonious coexistence of people who differ in race, language, and religion: a powerful message, a powerful model for Europe, for the world over.

The final score on April 18 was 2-2, after extra time.

The next day, April 19, 1938 (though it's not impossible that it was the 20th, or 21st, or . . .), there was a seemingly unimportant occurrence, one of the countless everyday occurrences that, in their banality, comprise the lives of human beings. One of the many degenerate (according to the Nazi aesthetic) painters, Paul

Klee, took a page from the April 19 newspaper and used that page, instead of a canvas, to compose a painting. The work is called *Alphabet I*. It is further described as "Schwarze pastose Wasserfarbe auf bedrucktem Zeitungspapier," or black paste on newsprint on cardboard. The newspaper was the *National Zeitung*, which, in February of that year—i.e., one month before the *Anschluss*—was seized in Vienna, along with the *Neue Zürcher Zeitung*. Paul Klee used page 13 (did Paul Klee believe in the magic power of numbers?), and this happened to be the sports page, the one reporting the results of the Final Cup from the day before. Klee, with swift hand, the hand of a divine thief ("Never has 'o' nor even 'i' been writ so quick"), his preparation for the painting entirely mental ("My tragedy is finished, all that is left to do is write it"), scrawled on that sheet of the *National Zeitung* a few letters of the alphabet, and a few hieroglyphics with the appearance of masks: signs of a "language no longer known"? The song of the birds, the flight of the sparrows, the language of the Spanish gypsies?

Klee is a master of color. Like many (many?) before him, he knows what color is. Even before 1938, he could well have made the same remarks to an observer that Vincent once wrote to Theo:

"But tell me, black and white, may they be used or may they not, are they forbidden fruit? Rembrandt and Hals, didn't they use black? and Velásquez???" (Vincent puts three question marks). "*Les vrais peintres sont ceux qui ne font pas la couleur locale*— that was what Blanc and Delacroix discussed once. Always and intelligently to make use of the beautiful tones which the colors form of their own accord, when one breaks them on the palette, I repeat—to start from one's palette, from one's knowledge of color-harmony, is quite different from following nature mechanically and obsequiously. Much, everything depends on my perception of the infinite variety of tones of one and the same family."

But here, in Klee's case, the point of departure is primary—not a canvas, but a page of newsprint that itself becomes a color. But forget color for now. Choose a page from the newspaper and look at it not to read it, but to use it for some simple, everyday purpose. Do you choose a page at random, or after a moment's thought? It's an easy situation to imagine. Take the most common example: a housewife. Take a common place: Danzig. Take a common woman: Johanna Trosiener. (Klee's catlike eyes widened a little.) Mid-morning, Johanna Trosiener looks up at the grandfather clock in the kitchen (or an hourglass, if you prefer), and says to herself—or rather, to the little one growing in her belly, she'll name him Arthur—she says to him out loud (or in her head): today it's going to rain, so I'm going to make potatoes. She grabs the basket of potatoes with the dirt still on them and then Johanna (by now, she's no longer Johanna Trosiener, it's no longer 1788, we've been deep in the twentieth century for a while now, the century of great innovations) goes to get the potato peeler and a newspaper to collect the peels. She opens the paper to get a page to lay out on the table. Her choice won't be totally indiscriminate, casual, even if its agent isn't yet Arthur's mother, even if she's far from believing in the equation *il pleure dans mon coeur* COMME *il pleut sur la ville*: can WILLING make it rain, make Jove thunder, God dawn, objects be imbued with pain? So no one is to blame, so unhappiness is immanent to life? So "Bagnacaval does well to have no sons." No, it won't be an unexamined choice. A twentieth-century Johanna

Trosiener, 99.9% of the Johanna Trosieners in the world, won't choose the obituary page. It's instinctively inappropriate to take the death announcements, the ink still "fresh" with the names of people who, in the early stages of decay, haven't even been nipped by the first worm yet, then crumple that potato-peel-covered page into a ball to toss in the trash. It's LIKE tossing yesterday's deaths in the trash. If, instead of the humble potato, dear to the humble Van Gogh . . . if Johanna Trosiener had WANTED to clean the floor, and now WANTS to put the newspaper on the floor, she'll be doubly mindful. You can't walk properly, or with impunity, on the obituary page, on graves, on the buried—on the dead.

Johanna Trosiener puts back the obituary page and pulls out another section. For her, any other page would be fine, one with bad (or good, depending on your point of view) news from Vienna—she has nothing to do, technically speaking, with politics. It takes her just a few minutes to read the local news—skimming the headlines is sufficient, on April 19 there's really nothing new, and like every other Monday, it's almost all sports. A Johanna Trosiener from Lugano sees out of the corner of her eye that at the Splendido (formerly Splendide, until the name had to be Italianized to protect the "italianità" of the Ticino) they show movies "100% *deutsch gesprochen*," and what else? A twenty-four-hour pharmacy? *Wille* wants us to all be in good health, long live *Wille*!

Yet not all, but many of the Johannas who live in the civilized places of the world, in Switzerland for example, have to take into account their husbands who, when they come home for lunch, before sitting at the table, grab the paper and flip through it, a bit anxiously, going straight to the sports page as always—he's a sporting husband, who Sunday after Sunday gets ready to give his support, his ration of cheers and whistles, to his favorite team. And there are other factors that a knowing housewife must take into account. There's the daughter who keeps up with fashion, the boy who does the crossword and rebus, and then the oldest, on the hunt for a job because the one he has is repulsive (that's how it is, it's not his fault—in the century after Arthur's, the century of Taylorism, work is often repulsive, or as he actually says, is shit!), is also looking for a room to rent because, as he says, he's sick of living in a zoo. *Et ceteri et cetera.* Life is made up of many things, the newspaper responds to all of them, it's the encyclopedia of the quotidian, and Hegel says—rightly so (even if Arthur Schopenhauer thinks Hegel is half charlatan)—that reading the newspaper is the modern form of prayer.

Did Klee have anything particular in mind when he chose the sports page of the *National Zeitung*? Or was it all the same to him? And the fact that it's page 13? It's highly unlikely that Klee would have let himself be persuaded by esoteric beliefs related to the number thirteen. But then, did Klee avoid page 5 intentionally? Five, in fact, weds the divisible number two with the indivisible number three. And in the masonic kabbalah, the number five indicates the female sphere: two is woman and three, the perfect number, is man. Five, a combination of the first even number and the first odd whole number, would therefore be the female element of the pair, the fertilized female, the number of Venus as the goddess of fertile union, of generative love, the archetype of creation. It took guts to think of creating a work of art on a day like April 19, 1938. A double five is nature's abacus: the fingers on both hands. In Roman numerals, X, which forms St. Andrew's cross, the two slopes of an hourglass, spokes on the wheel of time. Two fives (V: hands, funnels, tabernacles) meet at the vertex (X) and form a chalice, like in the poetry of the English Mannerists, great jugglers of the word, like Dylan Thomas: they form the Holy Grail. Its defining points make up the ideal design for planting. The archetypical nature of 10 manifests itself from decimals to decimations. Thus spake Zolla. Was Klee thinking of the decimations of the Jews, their imminent and radical elimination? And 13? Did Klee know that for a Baroque poet like Tasso the central pillar of a twenty-canto poem wasn't 10 but 13? It's impossible to say whether Klee was thinking about archetypes at the time. One can only make random guesses, which someone like Snoozy over here at the bar calls, without hesitation, idle, *nugae*, in Latin, before surrendering to the sleep that, like lead, presses down on his forehead and lowers his eyelids. Did Paul Klee follow sports? Was Paul Klee a reader of national and international sports news? You'd have to ask someone who knew him, his son for example. Otherwise, do as the historian does when he finds himself faced with something he doesn't know: say you don't know.

But this matter is inconsequential. Of great interest, on the other hand, is trying to give (give?) meaning to the signs, the hieroglyphics (from what depths they emerge) that Klee painted on that page of the *National Zeitung*.

– Mr. Klee! Can one speak of hieroglyphics without falling into heresy?

– Without falling into heresy! Klee replied, closing his eyes enigmatically, with the good-naturedness of a cat happy to show the good side of his feline soul.

One of the group, who worked at the Wind Factory (i.e., taught school), Mr. Window, the only one in the group wearing a tie, was instead preoccupied with the preoccupation of the formalists, for whom trying to confer significance on what resists significance is arbitrary. Like trying to break down a door when there's nothing to break down. The door is open.

But Klee calmed everybody down. The word "hieroglyphic" is a thrice-blessed word. It is in se and per se so infused with the sacred, with memory, with religion—we could rest easy.

Klee glanced over at Snoozy, laughing at the paradox. But the problem (as happens with all problems, to the delight of those who love to drink in company, gathered around the table at the osteria) remained unresolved.

– Take—it was Scribe O/17360's turn to speak—what appears to be the simplest sign to read in Klee's painting: Klee's O is the letter O, thirteenth in the Italian alphabet—another 13! Or is it a zero—or, more precisely, if you prefer, the mathematician Georg Cantor's aleph-0?

Could Klee's great O be a retort, a challenge? To Mondrian? Who knows! Curved lines, as says Ranuccio Bianchi Bandinelli— Arthur's *Wille* sent him a nice Easter egg for Easter: he was summoned to be Hitler's guide at the Uffizi when Hitler made his glorious *iter per Italiam* in the spring of '38, a few days after the April 18 Swiss Cup at the Wankdorf in Bern—anyway, curved lines, says Ranuccio, are charged with a unique sensitivity—easily calligraphic, and sensuous too. Snoozy cracked open his left eye. Whoever follows them is lost. A Dutch abstract painter fled Siena once he noticed that he kept seeing Duccio's angels on the street— alive, dressed as little girls. He was overwhelmed by their ovals.

Mondrian, inspired by Spinoza, completely focused on his own *Ethica Ordine Geometrico Demonstrata* from '31–32 on, achieved the perfect intersection of straight lines. Order and purity, centuries-old Flanders linen. Mondrian the Platonist, the chaste, the ascetic. The most Calvinist of the abstract artists. If he'd been a philosopher and not a painter he would have been capable of taking after Origen, blinding himself so as not to be distracted from his contemplations by women. By their ovals.

Lust for curves. And was Klee lost over them?

Klee laughed heartily, and in honor of the Mediterranean in general, of Siena and the Sienese Hills in Switzerland, threw back a good half-glass of Merlot, from Mendrisio. But Klee's O, what was it?

At first glance, yes, it's an O, a circle, but not a perfect one, no, no no no no, it's not Giotto's O—it wasn't made with a compass. Is it an O like a beat-up old ring, a jilted lover who took it out on a promise ring from the fair? A frame that got warped in the wasteland of refuse?

Interpreting an O is like interpreting a note on a trumpet, a solitary note that breaks through a pastoral solitude, in a trumpet concerto or Christmas oratorio, spurted out by a *tuba mirum spargens sonum per deserta regionum*, by a Stravinsky; and a furious hand turns off the radio, and there it lingers, in the dark, that single note, all night long.

In that most German night the blare of a horn made all the children, women, and elderly within range start in their beds. All the men were in barracks. They were expected on the field, as says the Mondrianesque Ariosto:

in groups of ten, twenty, four, seven, eight.

No one—save perhaps, by secret coordinates, Mondrian—protested the indecency of that honking sound coming from that black Mercedes. And anyway, the car had already taken off with a copious screeching of tire treads on the asphalt's grainy surface—until we meet again.

The degenerate painter Paul Klee, somewhere else on the famous page 13 of the *National Zeitung*, not far from the place he'd flung his fulminous O, had placed, as you can see, a timid H; maybe it was a rack, the kind you'd see in a gym, to which gym teachers, the kind who sleep with a whistle in their mouths, not exactly the favorites of the backwoods mountain kids who've moved to the big city, send the new guy fresh from the valley, already a bit hunched, awkward, dopey, like a hobo, a hick, with a peasant's limping gait; and they stick him up there on the rack to straighten out the damned spine on this Mediterranean peasant heedless of the Hellenism that should still be alive in him yet instead has been extinguished—by God, you'll learn to stand at attention like a real soldier and look people in the eye with a steely gaze. Like the guys in the Wehrmacht.

Then—after the Mercedes passed by with its blaring horn that not even a Stravinsky would have been able to imitate with the

Stravinskian intention of splitting the well-trained ears of gentlemen in tails, monsignors in purple, lovely ladies with rape-tempting décolletage in the blindingly bright concert hall—came a long silence in the long Germanic night. It was, that silence, deep in the heart of the night, the night of the heart without time, the *intempesta nox*: is it one in the morning? Two? Is it three, four, she wonders, tossing and turning, though she wouldn't switch on the lights for a million marks, a twentieth-century Arthur Schopenhauer's mother adrift in the Teutonic night without a lifeboat, without an Arthur, without help. And with her, all the plump, clumsy mothers of poor Little Tramps everywhere. Prison? Interrogation? Where? Where? God, God, *lama sabachthani*. Thinking, with boundless nostalgia, of the roar surging from the stadium, through the radio, when someone scored a goal.

Those were the days of peace, and a husband could, as the women would say (religiously), stick his head in the radio and follow the game, minute by minute.

– I don't know what they see in that thing, she would say afterward to a neighbor one Monday as they hung the laundry out to dry (oh, the linens of peacetime)—but my husband likes it too, it must be something.

These are the trifles that come to mind in times of war. Yet that was how men spent their Sunday afternoons during peacetime. Lying awake in bed, a twentieth-century Johanna Trosiener could pray to the wooden angel she'd bought before they came to disturb the peace in Düsseldorf—ask him to send more games, many more, every Sunday, with the stadium emptying out little by little, the streetcar ringing its bell at turns and intersections, bringing the men home from the match just in time for dinner. Yes, war is absence, loss of imagination.

Or was Klee's O the circumscription of a privileged space? The creation of a theatrical space—the theater!—of oblivion, yet also of openness for the viewer? But do visitors at the Zentrum Klee in Bern see it?

Snoozy wasn't the only one snoozing. Then a proclamatory voice in the desert insistently proclaimed: it is the space of a Greek or Renaissance temple. What kind of show do you want? One that incites the will to power? The pursuit of happiness? A sense of fatality? Of possibility? Or is it the temple that remains to be discovered, a place to be delivered to God so that He will return to dwell there? A dream?

Klee's O occupies a significant space. The black ink spares the Grasshoppers' lineup: Huber, Minelli, Weiler; Springer, Vernati, Rauch; Bickel, Rupf, Artimovics, Xam Abegglen, Chrismer.

The barkeep, as he was drying the glasses, went back to his question:

– Is it true that the Grasshoppers are completely financed by the Jews?

Whereas Klee's O had mutilated Servette, obliterating half of them, Servette who in fact would succumb inexorably in the rematch of the final—necessarily, one would say, fatefully, for lack of *Wille*. Was Klee thus the mere executor of a message that had come down to him from celestial space, from Iris descended through Bern's gray skies? Klee had traced the demolition, the cancer, that was to consume half of Geneva's lineup. The names erased belonged to the goalkeeper, the right fullback, half of the traditional center half and the left-wing halfback. Of the forwards, only the right wing's name was effaced. The survivors were the center forward, Belli (a Frenchman who, as such, was able in time to enjoy several months of hospitality in Germany's Stalag IV-F, as prisoner number 36293) and the left pair, Trello Abegglen and Georges Aeby.

Klee's most curious mutilation befell the inside right, Genia Walaschek. His name was erased above the waist, the line that demarcates the high and low energy fields, while Klee's fulminous gesture—Klee, the crimson Creator who flits here and there, squat like a sparrowhawk just alighted from its perch—spared the last part of the name: *schek*, the part that most recalls Masaryk and Beneš's poor Czechoslovakia—a foretaste of its fate, now that Austria's all in tatters.

Walaschek's name, split in half. You can see all of him from the waist down. With his eagle-soul flown away. The inside right's number 8 split in half and reduced to a 0.

– So Mr. Klee's O could be anything! the barkeep remarked abruptly from behind the bar. It could be one of those Japanese torture devices, from that Japan which, ominously, was sidling up to the Nazifascists of Europe. In the spring of 1938, a certain boy from the mountains, born on October 30, 1928, knew little or nothing—actually, nothing—of what went on in the world. There wasn't a book in the house, his only education outside of school came from his parents' osteria, from the regulars. Some brought in news, snippets of facts and commentaries; others contributed their own two cents before downing their glasses and going off on their way. One day, the carpenter was talking about different systems of punishment. Not all of them, he said: – Goodness no! He only knew some. Addressing the boy directly—because he was the only one who'd listen, because everybody else said that one drink was all it took, from one day to the next, to bring back his problem, that is, his being constantly and melancholically drunk—he said that one type of punishment was the Chinese method.

– You take a guy, he said, string him up like a salame and put him under dripping water. Like if you tie someone under the edge of the roof during Easter, when the föhn melts the snow day and night: one drop per second, right in the middle of the head. The strongest or the dumbest—idiots, imbeciles, retards, complete pinheads—could last a day, everyone else would go crazy within a couple of hours. And then another form of torture, a Japanese one, consists of taking a man, tying his hands behind his back, and putting a metal collar around his neck, a kind of bib with a nice sharp edge against the skin. They take the man into the middle of the desert and set him free. They tell him he can go wherever he wants. So he wanders around for a while in the boiling heat, then he tries to scream, cry out, sob, then pray, ask God for help, then he curses Him, and along with Him, the entire human race: the place, the time, the seed of their begetting and their birth.

Mr. Window broke in:

– Arthur is right. Where did Dante get the material for his *Inferno* if not from our real world?

The carpenter tolerated this interruption with oriental calm. From a poet named Giacomo Leopardi, he'd learned that human malice is the consequence of unhappiness and not the other way 'round. What an unhappy people the Germans must be! – At some point the blazing sun will take pity on him. With the help of hunger, of exhaustion, he'll stumble and that lovely round choker like a collar encircling a seventeenth-century nobleman's noble neck will cut off his head like his own personal guillotine. The carpenter also said (perhaps something of his own invention?) that one time there was a truck transporting poorly secured sheets of metal up a mountain road full of potholes and rocks. Then came a strong wind, the same kind that ruffles flags and women's dresses, and wouldn't you know it, one of the sheets flew off the stack and glided a stretch through the mountain air, like a giant's scimitar, a genie's magic carpet. Behind the truck a man in a sweater, sunglasses, and beret was zooming along on a Motosacoche, and the metal sheet slashed through the biker's neck like a razor before he could say ah or bah. He didn't even close his eyes. His razored head rolled like a ball down the slope, and the rest, the motorcycle and beheaded body, continued straight down the road until the bike, at the first curve, flew into the air—a man decapitated not by Klee's O but by a magician's flying dagger. Or perhaps Klee's O wasn't a Japanese torture blade, it was one of those car tires that fishermen on a certain island in the North put around the waists of those who've been sentenced to death for adultery . . .

– What's adultery?

With maximum tact and precision, as if he were inlaying a piece of solid wood furniture by hand, the carpenter explained the word adultery. Then he continued: – They put the condemned in the sea, upright. They put a light weight on the man's feet and tie the tire at his waist at just the right level so that the man floats vertically with his head above water. Then they stick a nice, shiny fish on his head. So a heron or any old sea bird with a hard beak will see the fish, nose-dive down to spear it, and, in doing so, with its long beak, split the adulterer's skull.

– What kind of places are these! said Asshat. Couldn't they keep things simple and just call Klee's O what it is: a zero?

Maybe yes. Klee seemed to agree, or so he seemed to be telling Walaschek and Co. He had to have heard of them—in 1938, in Paris, they were the national team who, under the leadership of Karl Rappan, the Wolf, inventor of the "bolt" tactical system, would face the great Germany of the wily Sepp Herberger, Hitler's Germany, which had reinforced both offense and defense with five greats from the Austrian Wunderteam:

Für deutsches Land das deutsche Schwert!
So sei des Reiches Kraft bewährt!

For German soil the German sword!
Thus shall the Empire's might be proved!

Lohengrin III.3

Yes, Klee declared, I've been labeled a degenerate artist by the swastika squad. I am one of those, I believe, who are convinced that the language of the German people must now be rebuilt from the ground up, making a tabula rasa of what the Nazis have pumped full of their drug. Germany has to start from scratch, from the *a priori* of reason if reason is what led to the sea of swastikas you saw waving in the wind before an enrapt Cologne as they celebrated one of their rites; if reason is also what led to the perversion of the pure meaning of words like *Blut*, blood, or *Boden*, soil. Words that in the eighteenth century were used to describe wines. We must start from zero.

– And what could all this have to do with me? Walaschek, worried, seemed to ask.

And Klee, laughing, seemed to reply:

– You were number 8, the inside forward. And I, by halving it and halving you, brought you back down to zero.

But Walaschek still had a reserve of fear somewhere deep in his eyes. The number zero makes people afraid. As if on the playground of a nursery or elementary school Klee had drawn a circle, an O, in chalk, and made all the children sit in a circle, then gave the teacher a look that said "ready." Upon which the teacher (a cute girl, really cute, nice right ventricle, nice left ventricle, nice little ears and upturned nose) said: – Now we're going to play Who's the Rotten Egg.

But when it was Bubi's turn—Bubi was the major's son who, when guests came to their house in Vienna (and this long before 1938), would raise his arm in salute like a little Hitler—Bubi dropped the handkerchief right behind little Sindelar. Sindelar was perfectly aware that the handkerchief was behind him, and that he was supposed to pick it up and chase Bubi and try to catch him in the space of one trip around the circle, otherwise he'd be the rotten egg. But he didn't pick it up. In three strides someone like Sindelar could catch every chubby Bubi, any child of those Third Reich beer-guzzlers, but it disgusted him to think of picking up that handkerchief that had been in Bubi's hand all the way around the circle—it was a big circle. So little Sindelar became the rotten egg and all the children, in their guilelessness, called out "rotten egg, rotten egg." Sindelar lied and said he was expected at home for something important, and stopped playing. Stopped forever. He couldn't play with Bubi or with the Grossdeutschland of Sepp Herberger and Hitler. He was found dead, from gas poisoning. Suicide—or revenge? Walaschek shuddered, as if out of the corner of his eye he'd glimpsed a leg-breaking fullback racing at him full of rage and malice. A zero? No. He wouldn't have wanted to grow up to be a good Genevan, all condo and office, like a good gasoline pump that pours gas into this or that tank without discriminating. He wouldn't have wanted to be a tree in a public garden or square with a railing around it, like a kid locked up in an orphanage or boarding school. Nor would he have wanted to spend every Sunday evening of his twenty years playing cards, because even if he had never read a single line of Arthur Schopenhauer, didn't even know who Arthur Schopenhauer was, he vaguely sensed that nothing lays bare the dismal side of humanity more than a game of cards, sensed that boredom is represented by Sunday, and necessity by the other six days of the week. Walaschek had found his place as inside forward, and he was happy because an inside forward is something more than an outside forward with his predefined role, running along the touchlines and toward the corner, crossing for goals. An inside forward has to have a complete view of the game, communicate with the other midfielders, pass not only to his own outside but also to the one on the other side with sharp cuts that confuse the other team's defense, or reach his own center forward with a long pass that won't end up being just a weak kick into the goal box, a Christmas present for the opposing goalie, handed over with kid gloves.

Bubi's handkerchief was foul, like Franz's sheets at boarding school, when Walaschek and Sindelar played hard in those teams on the outskirts of town, where they're tough, where a kid—and especially the most precise technical masters, like Sindelar and Walaschek—could really learn the ropes if he managed to keep the others (the types they call "butchers") from ruining his legs. One Friday evening, before the school's "guests" went to catch the train home for Christmas break, the housemaster inspected the dormitory. All the boys had to stand at the foot of their beds. When the housemaster got to Franz's bed, he reached his hairy white arm beneath Franz's pillow and with a brusque, deft flick of the wrist whipped back the white blanket and comforter, thereby revealing, *quod erat demonstrandum*, the bedsheet underneath, the hovel where that Jew-faced dog Franz slept. The sheet was filthy, and the housemaster, with crooked finger, summoned everyone to Franz's bed, and they all huddled around to get a good look at that dirty sheet. One of the boys, the youngest, was trying to see as much as he could from the second row by peeking through the bigger, more imposing bodies in front of him—just like during their soccer matches. The sheet was filthy. It wasn't blood, but yellowish stains, almost brown around the edges, as if, to pull another one on Franz, they'd cracked a rotten egg there. The youngest kid would later ask Rudolf—Rudi—who always knew everything, to explain. Because everyone had started snickering, nudging one another— though not like when a player is about to take a straight shot from eighteen meters and there are only a few opponents elbowing the defensive wall. Franz was the only one standing stock-still, he looked at his bed as if it were him there instead of the sheets, his unholy shroud desecrated with every second of that hell he had to endure. He looked on with his long face and his sad mouth, his lips prominent and fine like his mother's, so much so that, once, Zaccheo—the art teacher who outside of school was a painter and in class always talked about "our Pavolo Veronese," and if someone asked him what color to use he would reply "use your brain, Mr. So-and-So," since he was always formal with everyone—Zaccheo went right up to Franz, examined him with a cat's crafty eyes as well as a mountaineer's, and said to the entire class: all of Botticelli's women, even the Madonna, have mouths like this.

Genia Walaschek opened his eyes in the darkness. The housemaster, on the other hand, didn't know squat about Botticelli. But he did know how to play—just by tapping his squat fingers (in a digital version of the arrangement) with spirit and vigor—"Lili Marleen." Just lovely. Lili Marleen must have been the exact opposite of Bubi and Bubi's sort. There was something lovely about Lili Marleen, yes, the exact opposite of Bubi, who had even stolen two peaches that one of the youngest children hadn't allowed himself to eat so he could take them to his mother for Christmas. Bastard, thief, give those two peaches back, even if they're as hard as tennis balls, balls you could have played a little with, *con, avec, mit, sic,* as you're practically running through the passageways of the Bern station, returning, on the way, in a hurry, a flurry almost, obsessed with returning to the Klee Museum in Bern in time to see the *Schwarze pastose Wasserfarbe auf bedrucktem Zeitungspapier* again—running, almost, through the people in the long underpassages of Bern, packed with bustling crowds: and feeling like a kid with a tennis ball again. Captain Severino Minelli, only secondarily on the Grasshoppers, primarily fullback and captain for the national team, says that it's with a tennis ball that you learn to handle a soccer ball. Until you can control it like the balls or pins in and out of a juggler's hands in a variety show, in the circus—as if it's magnetized. When Sindelar had the ball at his foot, his caracoling advance, his advancing caracole, to the left, to the right, was so unpredictable that all his opponents watched him aghast, and, it must be said, with admiration and loathing. What would come of those movements, his body so gracefully aslant? The ball obeyed his choliambic foot like a dog, a tamed animal. Sindelar-Walaschek had only to don the tamer's cape and say *Hop Suisse, Hop Wunderteam*, and the ball would obey, like the Little Tramp with his cane or bowler. Sindelar (and Walaschek too) could shoot the ball into the corner (they call it the "set") of the opposing net just as he could (could, let's stop at could) have shot an arrow of spit into the swinish face of one of the Führer's men, a Bubi of *Anschluss*ed Vienna strongarmed and gassed. Old adolescent Vienna. But you can't die like Sindelar, otherwise we might as well all die. Ta ta ta ta.

Was that the trumpets of old Vienna or shots from a machine gun?

Becoming more serious than anyone had ever seen them before, Klee's grandmother and Walaschek's too, Jenny Morel, seemed to say, through Klee's mouth, to Walaschek:

– Try, when you play against Hitler in Paris, since *alles ist Politik*, our great Gottfried was right, try to make a divine play—*en surplace*, to push out, take down, reduce your Nazi fullback to the zero limit. We're against bullfighting, because we can't help but see

Him, Christ, in the bull—but use a toreador's style, feint in a way that throws your persecutor off balance, pull off a corner kick that surprises everybody and sends the ball straight into the net without anyone being able to touch it, which is the pinnacle for someone making a corner kick. You will be that pinnacle! If you have to make an eleven-meter kick (and you're so obedient that you wouldn't shy away from that enormous task, you've got a fanatical, or hostile, world watching you), you have to send the goalie one way and the ball the other, at mid-height. Every muscle in your body, and your brain too, even your heart, will have to cooperate.

– The *sophia* of the Greeks, Mr. Window cut in, is technique, art. The carpenter, the smith, the sculptor, the architect, and every other craftsman who knows his trade well, has his own particular brand of *sophia*; as does the singer, the musician, the fortune teller, the doctor, the poet. Try to find yours too, Number 8. It'll be your metaphysical experiment, a work in which the "disorder" of the self will reveal itself to be part of the divine order. It will be something that stands out—on the one hand, from the sphere, the ring ("my" ring?), of comedy, the theatrical space reserved for wild dreams and ordinary life; and on the other, from the tragedy of sacrifice. They'll put you on the degenerate team, along with Klee:

Grosz

Thoma   Schlemmer

Engelmann   Gropius   Feininger

Jawlensky   Walaschek   Klee   Kokoschka   Kandinsky

They make an especially tight attack with that slew of Ks like a bunker or a tank with cannons that could crack every tooth of the

Beelzebub Krauts of the swastika crew. A solid battery of Ks, and against them, in jerseys of virginal white, appear:

Treblinka

Göring   Goebbels

Auschwitz   Buchenwald   Mauthausen

Himmler   Eichmann   Hitler   Von Ribbentrop   Von Papen

Who'll be the first to stand up to the Third Reich?

What do they want anyway, these Swiss shits who come and cut us off right in the middle of 1938, and at the Parc des Princes, after the *Anschluss*, after we swallowed the Wunderteam? These Swissters, those pawnbrokers and watchmakers, produce their little shits with such passion and precision that you can never get them off the soles or sides of your shoes. But we'll make them eat their shit, every single piece, they'll get what's coming to them.

Instead of a round theater, a place of forgetting, of emptiness, of openness, what if Klee meant to draw a circus, a ring for elephants, horses, acrobats, clowns, with a thick rope around it to keep the performers separate from the audience?

The life of Genia Walaschek, of Czechoslovakian stock, before the stadium, began in the circus.

Walaschek's paternal grandfather was an orchestra director at a circus in Moscow, and Walaschek's grandmother-to-be worked at that same circus. The father of the future forward for the national team, a piano teacher at the Moscow Conservatory, chanced to marry a Swiss woman, the daughter of a watchmaker from the Canton of Neuchâtel who had gone to Moscow to ply his trade.

Skipping—with the speed typical of a civil registrar, always on intimate terms with his material: family trees and dates—skipping to the maternal branch, his grandfather is Swiss, his grandmother German, Jenny Toss from Hanover, destined to become, by marriage, Jenny Morel. Into this European hodgepodge, during the very years when Europe is in flames, Genia Walaschek was born in Moscow on June 20th in 1916. Between 1916 and '18, between the war on the German front, the start of the revolution, and the rise of Lenin, Russia was all a grid of sentimental journeys, as they're called by Viktor Shklovsky, someone who did his share of traveling down those roads:

– There was talk about some postman who ate his wife, said Shklovsky, but I don't know whether that's true or not. It was quiet, sunny, and hungry—very hungry.

And: – Our train carried coffins and on the coffins was scrawled in tar: RETURN COFFINS.

Even: – A rifle—especially a Russian one—is a treasure in the East. At the beginning of our retreat, the Persians gave two to three thousand rubles for a rifle; for a cartridge, they paid three rubles in the bazaar; for the same cartridge, they gave a bottle of cognac at the Kangarlu station . . . In Feodosia, a woman cost fifteen rubles used and forty unused, and she was yours forever. So why not sell a rifle!

The situation was getting depressing, especially for Walaschek. So Marina Tsvetaeva, with her incurable tragic goodness, asked:

– In Moscow? Were you born in Moscow? Where I lived in Moscow in the mornings the birds always sang, even in 1920 they sang, even in the hospital they sang, even in the middle of the crowds, they sang.

Then Marina too grew sad.

– During the Revolution, during the famine, all my dogs had to be poisoned so that the Bulgarians or Tatars, who had eaten worse, wouldn't eat them. Lapko avoided that fate because he went away into the mountains—to die on his own.

Whereas Walaschek went to Switzerland. At the beginning of 1918, his grandmother Jenny Morel and the young Genia (a year and a half old) left Moscow with a group of refugees. No coffins. The Swiss ambassador to Moscow, generously concerned about the child, added him to the grandmother's passport as if he were her own child. So as the son of Jenny Morel, Genia Walaschek arrived in his new home, the same Geneva of John Calvin. The mountains, for him, had parted. Although on May 10, 1926, Marina, yearning to see Rilke in Switzerland, Rilke who she was never to see, writes:

– Switzerland won't let any Russians in. But the mountains will have to move (or split!).

In 1918, the mountains moved.

Walaschek didn't see his parents, who had remained in Moscow, until 1964. In between, there's more than just the Stalin era. There's almost half a century. What does it mean to see people you were torn away from when you were just a little sprout, a bud, to see them again when you're forty-eight years old (at that age in Switzerland, you're still part of the *Landsturm*, the oldest group of military reservists) and your old parents are a generation older? People waiting for death, or to die together in some gloomy city apartment. Weighty words will be said: This is your father. This is your mother. And this is your son.

Things quickly take a turn for the excessive. Paternal and maternal solicitudes, tears. Kindness to the point of obsequiousness on the son's part. Which quickly brings on a veneer of irritation for the son, as someone who lives in comfort, in the modern, in the West. What is he doing there? There's always another tourist excursion: museums, Tolstoy's house, Herzen's, Chekhov's. The Bolshoi, in Red Square of course, with the long line for the Mausoleum. Caviar and vodka, yes. But it's another planet. After a few days it becomes clear to everyone that most men are like cats, not dogs: they're more attached to places than people. So it's best if they all return to their own beds, their routines. Swissair, Moscow-Geneva. He can't see the brother who was born after he left Moscow in 1918. That brother is dead.

He'd gone to the German-Russian front. At twenty. How many others like him? Hitler was a trainer who didn't tame animals but riled them up—young wolves, young tigers, he even drove the gentle elephants to frenzy. There were no more cages, protective ropes around the ring to protect the defenseless spectators.

So up to the age of ten, Walaschek grew up as a Morel and a Swiss. But a careless word on the part of his pretend-mother grandmother Jenny Morel, over which this woman from her place in the beyond is still mad at herself, going over it with a neighbor for the hundred-thousandth time, brings the Swiss ambassador's compassionate transgression in Moscow to light. Genia Morel regained the name Walaschek but lost his Swiss citizenship. He was given a Nansen passport for the stateless.

So Klee's O could also be a wheel, not the tire the fishermen in the North put around the adulterer condemned to death so that he floats vertically waiting for the deadly-beaked bird to crack his skull, but a third wheel, an old tire, an inflatable tube that in the cold season prostitutes on the edge of town burn in big fires that both sustain and beckon. You're the third wheel now, a voice kept saying. Just like that, Walaschek was off the national team, which played against Portugal on May 1, 1938. Then a loudspeaker made from fascist alloy filled the entire Milan arena and surrounding streets, in its fascistic timbre, with the names of the Portuguese players. A defense that, decasyllable with enneasyllable, sounded like the prelude to a madrigal:

Azevedo	Simoes	Gustavo
Amaro	Albino	Pereira

A legendary center forward, Peyroteo: a Mordechai of soccer, who always looks to his outside left, Cruz. The crowd saluted the Portuguese, fascistically, arms raised. The Swiss did not raise their arms and the audience in the arena hated those crude un-civilized butchers even more, though the Swiss names weren't without a certain musicality. But who, in that 1938 of perver-sions, in Milan, or in Bern on April 18 for the Swiss Cup final at the Wankdorf, who in the box seats or the nosebleed section would have thought that the names spared (the next day) by

Klee's paintbrush, the Grasshoppers', formed an almost eighteenth century incipit?

Huber Minelli Weiler
Springer Vernati Rauch
the blast of eternal winds
from rocky mines in flames!

The charm of a heptasyllable line, of names. A British poet took his turn to speak:
– Anyone who believes that the catalogue of ships (in Homer) is distant from (and distances us from) poetry understands nothing about poetry: he's a dimwit, no matter what scholarly laurels he may boast.

Ipso facto, he offered a prize (a carafe of red) to whomever, within five minutes, could come up with the most poetic team. That's exactly what he said: poetic. To everyone's surprise, and Klee's visible joy, it was the meat inspector. Who was hoisted onto a bench so that he could read his lineup. He seemed like a Petrarch beginning to declaim:

Rhone, Rhine, Iber, Seine, Elbe, Loire, Ebro

He took enough air into his lungs for a hendecasyllable-team:

iahn swan pučv; kuhn krol krick; han rahn cruyff schek tóth

and he hastened to explain that the schek at number 10 wasn't just some hypocoristic for Francesco: it was the inside forward for the Swiss national team, Eugene Walaschek, who the painter Paul Klee had split in half, April 19, 1938. Yes.

Everyone was momentarily absorbed in celebrating the victory of the winner of the carafe of red wine, but the jubilation ceased when an immigrant from the South thought it wasn't fair that he'd come in second. Sure, he had no more than a defensive trio, but still . . .

He jumped up onto the bench and began to recite:

Bacigalupo

Ballarin   Maroso

When on one postwar night Turin learned that their entire beloved team had been obliterated on the Superga hill, no one thought of the defensive line's names as being inscribed within a refined schema of Italian metrics: a hendecasyllable with an ictus on the fourth, eighth, and tenth syllables. Despite knowing nothing about meter, the unschooled loved to repeat, night after night, those names with their immanent mysterious charm. The unschooled don't know much about Dante, nor about a modern poet who loves goats "with Semitic faces," nor about the Triestina team, nor about Ariosto. But something settled beneath the entryway (the threshold) of the minds of the poor (like the keys to peasants' houses, in other times, might be stashed under a stone):

mi ritrovái   *per una sélva*   *oscúra*

e per la sélva   *a tutta bríglia*   *il cáccia*

mi stringerá   per un pensiéro   il cuóre

Bacigalúpo   Ballarín   Maróso

– Do the gentlemen agree?

Everyone turned toward Gottfried der Anti-Nibelung, in his aristocratic attire, who said amid the general silence:

– The word is the phallus of the spirit, centrally rooted.

– What does he expect people to know about the phallus of the spirit? some Knecht Ruprecht grumbled in his neighbor's ear, without daring to put his thought into the form of an official statement. However, it was agreed, without its coming to a formal vote, that it wasn't something people knew, but sensed. Ludovico Ariosto, on the other hand, he knew. From high up on a little cloud, still wrestling with additions to his poem, he would pick up ideas and rhymes from a café in some corner of Ferrara, enlisting new combatants for the siege of Paris:

Bacigalupo

Ballarin   Maroso

Otone   Avolio   Berlinghiero

Avino Trello Vonlanthen Walaschek Schiaffino

This for the audience. On the same paper as the secret plan for the procession on the eve of the match, for the finale of his octave, he composed three hendecasyllables, with the stress on the fourth, eighth, and tenth syllables: the ultimate defensive triangle, with a supporting rectangle, an offensive quadrilateral without fixed points:

Bacigalupo Ballarin Maroso
Otone Avolio Berlinghiero Avino
Trello Volante Walaschek Schiaffino

The barman reassured everyone: thanks to the Swiss National
Fund for Scientific Research along with a grant in the social sci-
ences, it would be scientifically demonstrated how, why, and
wherefore Roger Vonlanthen, an emigrant to Italy, had become,
scientifically, in the fans' mouths, Volante. Professor Syntax, for
his part, assured them all that Ariosto, a specialist in the *tourbillon*
(that is, a poetics *à l'hollandaise*), would rearrange the positions of
the four names in the defensive quad in every possible way until
he'd finally finished (or he'd had enough), and would recite it to us
full of *and*'s (which the people at the Swiss National Fund also call
a "polysyndeton"):

and Avino and Avolio and Berlinghiero and Otone

– When you've got the right stuff, said Gottfried der Anti-Nibelung, then you can take your first line from the train schedule and
the second from a prayer book and the third from a joke and all
together it'll still make a poem. And seeing that Klee had opened
his Siberian cat eyes all the way, he wanted to continue, but was
decisively interrupted by the barman, who had decided to bring
the discussion back down to earth:
– They didn't make him Swiss—Walaschek, I mean—because
of that game against Portugal, because of that spat between SA-

TUS (the Swiss Workers' Gymnastics and Sports Association) and ASF!

All the things you hear at the bar! Sports, weather, the rise in gas prices over the winter, pensions, and politics too: yes, politics, blown in as though upon distant wafts of wind.

– Who's that guy? Snoozy asked a neighbor, tired of these comments made just to cast doubt on the reigning harmony in the homeland.

– That's Knecht Ruprecht. He's a Nibelung too, naturalized Swiss. They say he's a sly one!

– He is, he is! Try and find a Nibelung who isn't. After '33 . . .

Snoozy was a little worried because his country was full of Nibelungs, naturalized or no. SATUS is in charge of sports and ASF controls soccer. Knecht Ruprecht added that they're as catty and jealous of each other as a couple of tarts. If ASF picked Walaschek, some newspaper, one of the ones put out by the Goths over there, prompted by SATUS, would publish a big headline:

COMMUNIST CELLS IN SWISS SPORTS

– Oh oh oh oh oh!

With the Fascists in full swing, they couldn't risk having Walaschek in Milan against Salazar's Portugal: Amadò, a citizen of Italian Switzerland, played in Walaschek's stead. Usually, a football player, if he's good (and Walaschek was good), has no difficulty getting documents and permits, whatever he wants. Take—said our friend behind the bar, a bullshitter of the more subdued variety—take the biggest publisher in French Switzerland. His name is Dimitrijević. One day (after the war), a certain Artimovics, a coach from Grenchen, a city dear to Mazzini, this Artimovics, who on April 18, 1938 was on the field at the Wankdorf in Bern as the center forward for the Grasshoppers against Trello and Walaschek's Servette (his name, like those of all the other Grasshoppers, spared by Klee's paintbrush), well, Artimovics makes an "appeal" for his compatriot Dimitrijević; Dimitrijević plays one game with Grenchen, as outside right, and boom, he's got a Swiss passport in his pocket—good-bye Tito and communism; he'll start a nice little publishing house. Our barman stopped there, and rubbed his hands with delight. But every rule has its exceptions. Walaschek, in a way, and for a long time, was just such an exception. Because of SATUS? An exception, that is (it's not pedantic to repeat), in the realm of soccer, because if we get to talking about farm workers or masons, workers in general, with them it's the rule. And thinkers? As early as 1933, Sigmund Freud wrote from Vienna to the (Swiss) minister (and colleague) Oskar Pfister: "Our horizon has been darkly clouded by the events in Germany. Three members of my family, two sons and a son-in-law, are looking for a new country and have not yet found one. Switzerland is not one of the hospitable countries."

– It's true, explained Mr. Vuilleumier, who was there by chance on a break from his work on one of our hundred thousand commissions, following some commissioners who'd left the room where General Guisan, from his portrait, kept an eye on everything. – It's true. The Helvetian authorities wanted to protect themselves against those waves of refugees. Since 1933 they had been trying to make Switzerland into a transit country rather than a land of asylum: in other words, they tried to prevent the refugees from

44

remaining by urging them on with strict sanctions, or even physically deporting them. The threats, boycotts, and acts of violence to which Jews as such were exposed weren't sufficient for them to be considered political refugees. In fact, anyone who clandestinely crossed the frontier but wasn't able to prove their political refugee status in a sufficiently convincing manner was sent right back to the nearest border post.

In 1938 (says Ernest Jones, a follower and biographer of Freud), the "inventor" of psychoanalysis "pointed out that no country would allow him to enter. There was certainly force in this argument; it is hardly possible nowadays for people to understand how ferociously inhospitable every country was to would-be immigrants, so strong was the feeling about unemployment. France was the only country that would admit foreigners with any measure of freedom, but on condition that they did not earn a living there; they were welcome to starve in France if they wished."

Those who were welcomed in Paris were countless. Thousands and thousands of children could have grabbed one another by the hand and made a nice big circle, as big as all of Europe, round like Paul Klee's O, and sung a nice "Ring Around the Rosie." Ring around the rosie—a pocket full of posies—ashes, ashes, we all fall down.

In the legions of those welcomed in Paris, the most numerous were perhaps the stray Russians, from Kerensky to Ivanov to the "noble" and non-noble of all kinds—all of them "fallen." In Paris, the Austrian émigré Joseph Roth was actually dying. Of hunger—perhaps not for bread, but for everything. Alcohol took care of the rest. A kind-hearted waiter, as Roth sat at his table (at the Café

Tournon) penniless and wasted, considerately asked the unfortunate, hard-up writer:

– *Quelque chose pour commencer, monsieur?*

– *Je ne commence plus, je finis.*

And back in Russia, Osip Mandelstam was *fini.*

Every so often, a voice, quietly, would ask Scribe O/17360:

– And after death?

– After death I too will go down, as everyone does, into Hades. I'll wander among the shades looking for my mother, then I'll wander around some more, through the fields, looking for Heloise and Tsvetaeva, with her tearful eyes, perhaps Helen of Troy too, or Marilyn, or Phryne, or Rembrandt's Bathsheba, or Poussin's Venus . . .

– And then what?

– Then nothing.

She stood at the entrance, her eyes full of tears, aged, almost gray, hands crossed on her bosom. This was soon after the murder of Ignace Reiss in which her husband, Efron, was implicated. She stood as if infected with plague: no one approached her. Like everyone else I walked by her.

No, Berberova didn't care for her. Marina's eyes. "Each socket seemed a ring without a gem." Like Klee's O.

Now nobody asked leave to speak, everyone just chimed in. Herzen turned to Bakunin and said vehemently:

– You have to open man's eyes, not gouge them out.

Klee's O could be the eye of a cat who remembers having once been a tiger. The eye of a leopard. Klee's eyes gleamed.

– Of a Leonardo. Is it true that Leonardo would buy birds at the market to set them free? If he'd been alive in the twentieth century, he'd have sold all his Mona Lisas to buy the Jews and set them free. To buy land for the Palestinians and set them free.

– Long live a free Palestine!

Mr. Window asked abruptly:

– But have you ever seen a cat's eye? It fla . . . He broke off mid-flash. He liked Klee's game, cutting words and names in half, as with Walaschek.

Whereas Mr. Snoozy, who did not appreciate names cut in half, responded, as if at Mass:

– Ashes—flashes.

Klee's eyes lit up.

– Fel . . .

– Felix? Feline.

– I don't understand why people aren't speaking in complete words all of a sudden, complained Mr. Snoozy, who had been to Berlin, and, as he went on to say for the three-hundredth time now, in 1930s Berlin you could leave your umbrella leaning against the wall at the train station, come back an hour later, and find it right where you'd left it.

For his part, my neighbor on the left reasoned:

– That thing with Paris, their not allowing the foreign-born to engage in any lucrative enterprises, I don't understand it.

"And behold, one shade from the depths of her head turned her eyes toward me . . ." Was it the eye of a mangled murder victim relegated to the cloisters of hell? Was it the eye of Sindelar (who will be called, when *rien ne va plus*, "the Mozart of soccer" in the *Encyclopedia of Modern Sport*), trained on the gas stove? The star of the Wunderteam was burning out. He re-

fused—as confirmed by official sources, trustworthy sources—
to play for Greater Germany. Was he overcome with synderesis,
a crisis of conscience? He was found in his house, dead. That
"mid-month moon," for him, would never come again, when
the girl (Pindar's) would "unbind for the hero the fair girdle
of her virginity"—never again. All that was left for him would
be the nauseating smell of gas that, to a Swiss, neutral, aged
ten in 1938, could only faintly recall the smell of the makeshift
military latrines at the edge of town. And a scribe like O/17360
would really have to ask Marina to explain her comment that
"one mustn't forget that all poets of the world have loved soldiers." She'll explain it to him in the afterlife, whither she de-
parted from Yelabuga on August 31, 1941, by way of a nice slip-
knot. Sindelar killed himself too? someone asked, in secret, in
Vienna. Was Klee's O a ring that had lost its finger? The finger
of a bride, of a bishop extending his hand to the faithful. A hundred thousand people kiss a bishop's ring, a hundred thousand
are happy. And maybe even the germs celebrate. God's finger
touches Adam's—and life is created. Was that a good idea? Or
it's God's finger that crushes him, Adam. But neither Michelangelo nor Masaccio deem it important for God to wear a ring like
a pope or a bishop. Or is it Hannibal's ring? He kept it to hide
poison under its stone.

Or were they the eyes—rings without gems—of Freud's four
sisters? Having no prospects for maintaining them in London,
Freud had had to leave his four elderly sisters, Rosa Graf, Dolfi
Freud, Mitzi Freud, and Pauli Winternitz, in Vienna, but when
the Nazi danger drew near—Jones specifies—he and his brother

Alexander gave them the sum of 160,000 Austrian schillings (about $22,400 dollars) which would suffice for their old age, provided that the Nazis did not confiscate it. Toward the end of the year Marie Bonaparte endeavored to bring the sisters to France, but she failed to get permission from the French authorities. Freud had no special reason to be anxious about their welfare, since the persecution of the Jews was still in an early stage. Fortunately, he never knew of their fate; they were incinerated some five years later.

What was Klee thinking about as he was painting his (not Giotto's) O, the O that cut the name of Walaschek in half, decapitating him? Was he thinking of that fierce inhospitableness? On March 28, 1938, seventeen days after the arrival of Hitler's troops in Vienna, three weeks before the Swiss Cup final at the Wankdorf in Bern, the Federal Council decided that visas would be required for Austrian passport holders, visas that were promptly granted to Austrians entering Switzerland for commercial or industrial purposes and refused to everyone else. If someone had relatives or assets here, the case was turned over to the federal Foreigners' Police. After an accord with Berlin, the passports of all non-Aryan German citizen refugees had to bear the letter J.

Mr. Vuilleumier, with a certain confidence, but tact as well, brought his mouth to Scribe O/17360's ear—clearly he wanted to share a secret:

– Did you know about this? The secretary of the Writers' Society, being questioned by the Foreigners' Police any time between 1938 and 1939 about possibly granting a German or Austrian writer temporary residency, acted no differently than someone in any other profession or union, the working classes included. Yes, they were capable of being charitable on occasion, but still they were out to protect the interests of their own.

– And may our writers have long and happy lives! Scribe O/17360 blurted out. Klee looked at him, curious. Once again he seemed the crimson Creator circling like an owl looking down at the shoddy world he has just (in the year 1934) created, and then going back to rest on his perch, pouring himself a whisky, maybe paring his nails a little. Why should Klee have been thinking of those dying of starvation or gas or torture in 1938? After all, he was painting, working with colors. Perhaps he was like a child looking for a piece of candy in one corner while his mother, who hid it in the opposite corner, knitting and smiling, indulgently guides him: "Cold, cold," which is to say: you're way off base. Ernest Jones is instructive in this regard:

"So my first act on reaching London on March 22 was to obtain from Wilfred Trotter, who was on the Council of the Society, a letter of introduction to Sir William Bragg, the famous physicist who was then the President of the Royal Society. I saw him again the next day and he at once gave me a letter to the Home Secretary. I was taken aback at discovering, though not for the first time, how naïve in worldly matters a distinguished scientist can be. He asked me: 'Do you really think the Germans are unkind to the Jews?'"

But it's likely (or certain) that Klee was well aware. Klee didn't live on the innocent isle of England. He'd been acquainted with the Nazis since the thirties and, when they took power, upon his return to Switzerland to seek—in vain—citizenship there, he got to know them even better. Someone who between 1932 and 1934 painted *Mask of Fear*, *The Scholar*, and *Angst*, is someone who knows. "The more horrible this world (as today), the more abstract our art, while a happy world brings forth an art of the here and now. [. . .] I have long had this war inside me. This is why, interiorly, it means nothing to me. [. . .] I remain in this ruined world only in memory, as one occasionally does in retrospect."

Maybe Klee's O was an O long and hoarse, the kind that comes over the stadium when the ball, from the edge of the box, after the player has—with intent, with will, with muscular force, with his foot—infused it with power and dynamic tension, flies past the barricade of defenders, goes just over the crossbar, or more dramatically, hits the crossbar, the goalkeeper stranded? Yes, it could be a collective expression of pain or remorse, which then makes the outpouring of joy when the ball hits the net so much more unrestrained, and the teammates run to embrace the man who struck it with victorious force. To embrace the player who is still running with his arms up toward the crowd in the stands behind the goal, up toward the sky and the gods. Those who live on Via Leopardi in Naples say that when Maradona scores, their houses shake from the roar of the crowd.

At the mention of Leopardi, who possessed perhaps the most sensitive ear in the world, Schopenhauer wanted to sneak in what he called one of his "little thoughts":

– I have long been of the opinion that the amount of noise which any person can bear undisturbed stands in inverse proportion to his mental capacity, and therefore may be regarded as a fairly decent measure of it. Therefore, if I hear the dogs barking for hours together in the court of a house without being stopped,

I know what to think of the intellectual capacity of the inhabitants. Goethe in his last years bought a house which had fallen into disrepair close to his own, simply in order that he might not have to endure the noise that would be made in repairing it.

With the air of a lawyer at trial, Schopenhauer looked around to assess the effect of Goethe's purchase, but he ascertained that Tsvetaeva hadn't even cracked a smile, nor had Joseph Roth.

So Snoozy threw out another name:

– Beniamino Gigli!

Yes, just as Maradona could make the houses on Via Leopardi shake, Beniamino Gigli's voice could shatter a glass an armlength away, like the waves of wind that caused the new (in 1940) bridge in Tacoma to collapse. The wind blew at the same harmonic frequency (with the same character) as the bridge itself, thus creating resonance and making it oscillate too much, until the bridge at last gave way. A harbinger of the end of the world, when the hour of the abomination comes? When will the wave vibrating at the same frequency as the world arrive? What about those choruses at night in Nuremberg, with thousands upon thousands of flags and swastikas?

Walaschek's favorite memory from his soccer career (he played twenty-six or twenty-eight times with the national team) was the double-header against Greater Germany, in Paris, for the World Cup. Walaschek, who hadn't been able to play against Portugal in Milan (Italy had protested Walaschek's selection, given that his application for naturalization was still being processed), got FIFA's approval for Paris. Once FIFA recognized (fourteen votes in favor, ten against) Walaschek's Swiss-soccer citizenship, Jules Rimet, the "inventor" of the World Cup, could say that soccer naturalized Walaschek before the country officially did.

The first match ended in a tie, and the rematch took place on June 9, 1938 at the Parc des Princes. With the *Anschluss*, Germany and Austria formed a single team, and at the twenty-second minute of the first half Goliath-Germany was already ahead two to zero. But David and his slingshot repeated the miracle. Walaschek initiated the comeback, Amadò brought them to a tie, and then came Trello Abegglen's two goals. Did news of the great match in Paris make it to Moscow? Certainly not. Did the grandfather and grandmother in Moscow, orchestra director for the circus and circus employee, know about their grandson in the West who instead of taming horses or elephants, being a trapeze artist or acrobat, juggled a soccer ball for the Swiss national team? If Juno had decided to bring the message to the grandmother in her corner of the circus (though in 1938, during Stalin's purges, was the circus still running?), perhaps she would have started spurring on the horses (since animals are polyglot) with a "hop Suisse!" and the grandfather, directing the orchestra, would have slipped a few notes from the Swiss national anthem into the triumphal march at the finale, just as Tchaikovsky had done with "La Marseillaise" in the *1812 Overture*.

Perhaps Klee's O was the oval destined for Sindelar, for his grave. He was the star of the Wunderteam, but he refused to play with the white shirt and the black soul of Hitler's Germany, and one day was found dead in his house, extinguished by gas. Suicide? Revenge made to look like suicide? One of the great forwards "of all time" was dead, but all of Austria was dead too, and no one on the

Wunderteam of writers could, like Pindar or Homer, sufficiently honor that geometric weaver of intricate patterns with a leather ball. Thus the tombstone's oval would remain empty, it too a ring without its gem; and so, an old Walaschek, fifty years after the victory over the Germans in Paris, on his way from Bern to Geneva, his home, on the InterCity train (there'd been a reunion of the old glories—the remaining survivors with gray or sparse hair, wool vests, Walaschek with a cane for his achy hip—to commemorate Rappan, the old fox, the coach of the miracle; they'd made several toasts, posed for group photos, for TV cameras), and so, on the train, on his way home, he dreamed up a team that was all offense, apologizing to the Czechs and Belgians and Dutch and then a little to everybody, to the English greats too (but we also beat them in '38—that's Walaschek's second favorite memory) because he had to leave them out of the ideal team, there where the divine act floods the universe, penetrates all living things, submerges them: wherever they may be, it is; it precedes them, accompanies them, follows them. One must simply surrender to its waves:

Zamora (or Plánička?)

Di Stéfano   Puskás

Pelé   Falcão   Schiaffino

Sindelar   Walaschek   Meazza   Eusébio   Mortensen

He could have made up a hundred ideal teams in his dreams, and he addressed everyone, included and excluded, with the informal *tu*; for instance, apologizing—I'm sorry, having to leave someone like *tu* out. Players, both teammates and opponents, had always and spontaneously addressed one another informally. No soccer player in the world would have been able to hold back his laughter (Walaschek was laughing, in his sleep, on the Bern-Geneva InterCity) upon reading (exactly on April 19th, 1938, on the exact day printed at the top of the page 13 of the *National Zeitung* that Paul Klee tore out to paint his alphabet, his sacred incisions made with a black-dipped paintbrush over Genia's printed name, obscuring, like an impetuous wave in a stormy sea, his "Wala") the proposal-injunction in the *Giornale d'Italia*, immediately reprinted in the other newspapers in the civilized world ("syphilisation!" Ulysses yelled in Dublin), that "all letters to figures in public service wherein the formal *Lei* is used instead of the preferred formal form *Voi* shall not be answered. *Voi* has also been fully adopted in the armed services."

Voi, Captain Severino Minelli. The Captain of the Swiss National Team, Severino Minelli, evidently of Italian origin, and along with him the midfielder Sirio Vernati, perhaps aggravated the violently anti-Swiss, pro-Salazar Milanese fans even more, since it was precisely those two deserters who were the first to refuse the Fascist salute, whereas Salazar's Portuguese were all too happy to oblige, from Azevedo to Cruz, the outside left. The Fascists in Spain were just a few kilometers from the coast; Daladier had recently succeeded Blum, the director of the Vienna State Opera; Bruno Walter had been dismissed, the Austrian bishops had recognized the *Anschluss*, a journalist for the *Berner Tagwacht* was fired over an offensive article about Hitler . . . In the group photo from Milan, Captain Severino Minelli had a grim look, like William Tell with Gessler.

Things go even better in dreams than they do on computers, which, in addition to being able to put together the ideal concert, will be able (in the year 2000 . . . ?) to "copy" the best plays of the great champions, "reinvent" them, put them into different "contexts," put a player on the field with players from other eras. The impossible game, the Platonic ideal of soccer, shall soon be possible. In the arena of Genia Walaschek's dreams, though, it was already happening. Maneuvering his words delicately, as if dancing on tiptoe, feinting, he conferred with Sindelar (as *tu*) to set up "golden head" Kocsis, who was right in front of the goal, poised to shoot into the top corner—even Plánička wouldn't be able to stop a shot like that. He dreamed of the pleasure, with a dash of fear and trembling, when, near the flag, under the linesman's watchful eye, he would go for a corner kick. He didn't glance at the packed arena, the crowd facing him or the crowd behind him, the grandstand; there were people cheering and heckling, with anthems and curses, whistles and applause, almost as if all human suffering and thirst for glory had been relegated to those open mouths from the four cardinal points of the world. You'll go for the diagonal shot, not too close to the goalie, not too far back—it should come out like a constellation of stars on a clear winter's night, like Orion's club; first there must be the mental calibration of impulse, power, and skill, so that the ball, parabolically aslant, perhaps ricocheting like the quotidian gossip and backbiting of life, meets Trello's head or Aeby's foot; and in the name of Switzerland, may God confound Germany. God (no, this isn't taking His name in vain) help us, may He give the ball an anomalous unpredictability. Enlighten Trello so that he chooses the right moment to break free, to soar up. Luck, as with everything, matters. A goal can be a miracle, can verge on the banal or verge on the sublime. And the stadium entire, like a microcosmic humanity, can rejoice in it. O, the disappointment when the ball doesn't make it into the goal. Going home at night and sitting on the train, staring down at your banged-up shins.

Klee's O could be the oval idea of an ordered cosmos, the annual ring on a transversal section of a tree trunk, halfway between roots and leaves, in a continuous cycle. Klee showed them a pink circle on a section of an old larch. – Here I was born, and there I died. Then with the pencil he marked another circle, two millimeters wider. – But the tree doesn't know—you took no notice!

– The cosmos of form, Klee tells his students at Bauhaus, itself an expression of religious sentiment, resembles creation so closely that only a breath is needed to bring it to life. Or perhaps the O is a container of seeds, an assemblage of stages of growth: an archetypal egg—a musical note.

Or is it a magnifying lens? The rim of a pan? Nadezhda Mandelstam said she went around Russia with Osip's poems hidden in pans. Then she decided to memorize them for fear that the authorities would take them from her. Perhaps it's a ring on which to dock the ship of life? Is it, in the gray fog of the *National Zeitung*, the pale (black) sphere of the sun? Or God's signature on Ulysses's diabolical question-challenge?

Three times it turned her round with all the waters . . .

Alain de Lille, the platonic theologian, to whom Dante also refers, says that "God is an intelligible sphere, whose center is everywhere and whose circumference is nowhere." Is Ulysses's ship, swirling in on itself three times, meant to imitate the signature of God? Or is it a serpent, symbol of eternity, curling into a circle (putting its tail in its mouth)?

Is it the first circle of Hell?

Klee raised his hand. Head bowed, he said:

– Cheer up! Value such country outings, which let you have a new point of view for once as well as a change of air, and transport you to a world which, by diverting you, strengthens you for the inevitable returns to the grayness of the working day. More than that, they help you to slough off your earthly skin, to fancy for a moment that you are God; to look forward to new holidays, when the soul goes to a banquet in order to nourish its starved nerves, and to fill its languishing blood vessels with new sap.

Where to dock the ship of life? A soccer player's ship speeds toward algae-filled waters, the lacustrine trash dumps of coves. In Walaschek's time, in Switzerland, only two or three teams earned enough to put food on the table. In 1938, for the three world championship matches, the players got 133 francs each. At the age of thirty or even before, they send a soccer player to Serie B; at thirty-two he's an old nag, and it's rare for him to get any field time, perhaps only if he trains diligently, doesn't drink, doesn't smoke, has a wife who, Penelope-like, shrivels up in the exercise of pure fidelity, and because he's a good strategist, plays with his head and makes the younger ones do the running. But then it's over. And there's nothing left for ex-players but going to the stadium to watch other people play. Stare at them on the television, when television comes. There's still the chitchat at the café. The ex-player can only talk. Experience the form. Life is over; all that keeps him afloat is the ephemeral wisdom of life. He loses himself, happy to be lost, in the sports pages, as others lose themselves in card games, Jass or Scala Quaranta. For a painter, a poet, a sculptor, it's completely different. When Paul Klee grabs page 13 of the *National Zeitung* to make his marks—the O that decapitates Walaschek, who on April 19, 1938 wasn't even twenty-two years old—he, Klee, is almost sixty, having been born on December 18, 1879 in the Canton of Bern. He can feel his life coming to an end. In his last days, he seeks help from the tonic sun of the Ticino (where he will die on June 29, 1940, at the Sant'Agnese clinic in Muralto), and when he gets there something mournfully cheerful happens that confirms the difference between a football player and an artist. The artist is generally a fire that burns slowly and can singe anyone who comes near for centuries. Not so the soccer player—he has to do whatever he can in a hurry, burning with a bright but short-lived flame, like the bonfires on Swiss National Day, August 1st, made with tree branches and dry twigs—fleeting. In 1938, a federal councilor was officially present in the stands to keep an eye on the soccer players who gathered for the cup final—the ritual could no longer go unobserved. The Federal Council, our government, sent the winners in Paris, who had beaten Nazi Germany, a heartfelt telegram on behalf of the Swiss people. When Klee is forced to leave Germany and return to Bern, his native canton, due to the rise of Hitler, only a few connoisseurs appreciate him; sure, Picasso and Braque come and visit him, but all in all Klee is considered an eccentric, a madman—the well-meaning popular conclusion is a fair one.

One day, then, Klee comes to Minusio, near Locarno. To put his affairs in order, they send him to a teacher, a father of many children, a local historian, and quartermaster in the army. A quartermaster has to see to the troop's lodgings, its sustenance. Even when he's not in uniform, the quartermaster is still a quartermaster: he's competent like no other, and active in over thirty units or associations of public interest. He knows everything about the institutions of the "Rechtsstaat": he knows it in theory and practice. He always brings theory down to reality, and vice versa. Even if, given his many children, the conversation were to touch on a theme presumably quite beyond his interests—that is, love—he wouldn't diverge from his methods. Paternally, addressing Scribe O/17360, he confers order upon the world: – You want to know, my friend, what love is? Love is: A . . . B . . . C . . . With his right index finger he counts off the elements of his Logos on the out-spread fingers of his left. His right hand always knows what his left is doing. Another fascinating thing about him is the fact that he looks like the twin, face- and build-wise, of Doctor Clitterhouse (*The Amazing Dr. Clitterhouse*, by Anatole Litvak, also from 1938), i.e., Edward G. Robinson.

When Klee went to see him, the quartermaster Dr. Clitterhouse helped Klee just as he would have helped any other child of God. Artists are always in need of help. Artists always have their heads up in the clouds. He, on the other hand, was a regular guy with his feet on the ground. One day Klee opened a folder containing several drawings in black and white and in color and in watercolors in front of his patron Edward G. Robinson, and humbly, simply said: – Help yourself!

– Help myself? No, thank you—that stuff? No!

Klee, unruffled, closed the folder and, like Manfredi in Purgatory, presuming that Dante should recognize him, said smiling:

– You, sir, are a great and wonderful man, but when it comes to art . . .

Today the quartermaster could calculate the value in francs, dollars, yen, of that madman's drawings, his watercolors, that he refused at the time. Someone more provident, more shrewd (Arthur's—Arthur Schopenhauer's—ears perked up, intrigued by this detail), turned out to be the mail woman from the neighboring town. There was always some "artist" from the North in that area, and not just in Ascona among the loonies at the Monte Verità commune. If she delivered an express letter, a telegram, or some money, and a person started to give her a tip, she would stop him, kind but firm. And she would pull a little album out of her mailbag.

– If it's not too much trouble, just put a sketch, just a scribble, in here.

The painter, amused and flattered, would leave a "scribble." As if a little girl had asked a Walaschek to do a half-dribble right there in her front yard. That's it? But she sure got herself a collection that today . . .

– What does Walaschek think of Paul Klee? —the quartermaster asked.

– What do you expect him to think? Is he a soccer player or isn't he? Arthur burst out vehemently, as he happened to do quite often. This time even Snoozy raised an eyebrow at the philosopher. Are athletes not allowed to think? But yes, Walaschek probably didn't think anything of Klee. Maybe he knew a little more about him than he did about Pontormo (about whom he knew zilch), since Klee's name came up in the paper every now and then . . .

But is this knowledge? Let's try reversing the question: What did Klee think of Walaschek? Between 1938 and 1940, they were two "constellations" that hadn't met. It's not outside the realm of possibility that Klee's rapacious eye had come across, by chance, the letters constituting the name "Walaschek"—although not when composing *Alphabet I*: there the erasure of half the name is the product of *Wille*. One could presume that on April 19, 1938 Klee didn't read the story on the final between the Grasshoppers and Servette—he was only aware of having in front of him a page from the newspaper concerning sports. Or the question might be: What do people, more than half a century later, think of Walaschek? To anyone under the age of sixty, the name means nothing. Zero. Here's where the O comes back in. The thirteenth letter of our alphabet? Omega? The end, or zero, null, the ultimate stop sign?

It was a somewhat embarrassing moment, so to distract the assembly, Scribe O/17360 said:

– Listen to this: just yesterday I come out of one of the thousand banks around here where I'd cashed a check for half a million lire from one of my little scribblings, and who do I see? You'll never guess, so I'll tell you. I see Selmoni, Pierino Selmoni, he's standing there like an undercover agent observing the public's reaction to the column in front of the main entrance that the bank commissioned him to sculpt. Maybe it's not Trajan's Column, or the one in Place Vendôme, but it's a nice, honest column that goes from a square base to a cylindrical peak, with a progressive increase in the number of sides on each section—from four to infinity. A beautiful play of geometric rupture and continuity, past and future, tradition and innovation, Anchises and Palinurus—it's by restoring tradition that art shows itself to be revolutionary, as Gide says about Poussin. Then Selmoni starts laughing like only he, round and good and clever, knows how, because, as he says, verbatim: "I've been here for three hours watching these good people, and it's like my column has always been there, for centuries. As if everyone has always known it was there. Or as if it weren't there at all, a mirage. They don't see it, they haven't seen it, they pass right by. If fifty years from now someone were to convince people—whether he himself believes it or not, that doesn't matter—convince people that it's a masterpiece, is able to get it into some travel guide with a star or two, there'll immediately be ten tourists from the North who come looking for it, then twenty, then a hundred, then everyone will stop at it and take videos and pictures of themselves in front of the column. Just like they go to the Pisa baptistry to hear the 'famous echo,' they'll come here to be able to say they stood next to 'Selmoni's column' . . . "

A perfumed lady who seemed to have only just freed herself from the coiffeur of her blonde tresses called us to order:

– We were talking about Mr. Paul Klee, about his O!

– Right, our friend at the bar said. Is it the frame of a mirror without the mirror? The rim of a well with no well? A dark well? Or the black hole, the commencement, the coronation of the "gouffre"—the vortex, the "immense horrible abyss"—of the unfathomable?

– A dark well? Oh, come on! Let's keep out of the gutter, let's not compete with toilet maids and lavatory lackeys.

Klee smiled for a moment, a bit Tartarlike, and his eyes darted around like Mephisto's on the lookout. The mouth of a well? That might be true for journalists who, in keeping with their journalistic superficiality as butchers of language, which our friends Schopenhauer and Nietzsche (Schopenhauer and Nietzsche each gave a brief, deferential nod) tirelessly denounced, especially if writing about someone like Walaschek—without a second thought. They would say that he played 28 (or 26?) games on the national team, that he made 103 goals, that the game against England was the ninth in his career, that he played for the first time on the national team in 1937, the last in '45; and some of those journalists, those plagues of language (with Nietzsche as witness) would go so far as to extrapolate—and would think in so doing that they'd reached the bottom of the well—that since he was active in those years, in terms of presences in the nationals, or rather, "presence fees," the war had disadvantaged someone like Walaschek, just as it hadn't favored other "exponents" of sport, Coppi and Bartali for example. But never would it cross the mind of a single one of those bloodsuckers to include among the deductions in the account of someone like Walaschek anything like the death of an unknown brother or a lonely, faraway city, Moscow; in Hanover, what kind of hearts they, the relatives of his grandmother Jenny Morel, have beating in their chests, what they think of the great Führer who calls up schoolchildren and sends them to the slaughter. He sells their still-living flesh. Those journalists who journal about sports don't even hit the epidermis: they don't even reach the opening of the well. If we still want to talk about them.

– No, shouted a woman in the second-to-last row, now that they have computers and can play on them like my grandson does, they'll do a full profile on him, they won't even leave out his shoe size, and how many assists he made, how many fouls he had, the number of times he even touched the ball. *Madamina! Il catalogo è questo.* If Don Giovanni came back to tour the sheets of Europe, what a treat it would be for computers. How many ejaculations here, how many there; they'd even calculate the hourly speed (of ejaculation). Pelé got up to 1003 too. The record. They claim to count, to calculate everything.

A former coach, then masseur, and finally bookkeeper for the local team was thinking his own thoughts; his head was in his hands, his elbows firm on the table. – God, they called them "presence fees." For those games against Hitler's Germany they earned 130 francs each, and that because an anonymous donor came forward. Today they would get, or expect, a thousand, ten thousand times more. One hun-dred and thir-ty francs! A gesture void of any form of elegance or respect whatsoever. Or style! But can Switzerland have style?

The baker jumped to his feet, red in the face, Swissly flushed.

– Did you say a thousand times more? Did you say ten thousand? That's an insult to those of us who work for a living. But those idiot workers who have to walk the streets like whores to feed their children, they get all excited when they find out that their sports stars are paid what they're paid. The more they get paid the happier they are. This is something we've learned from America—we copy all the idiotic things they do. There, people show off how much money they make like monkeys show off their penises to compare size.

The blacksmith, who used a bellows from Shakespeare & Company, declared the moment he set foot in the osteria that ninety-nine percent of people have more wax in their ears than brains in their heads.

The ex-masseur wanted to specify:

– Walaschek was right within the average: he handled the ball well, he was hardy, too—they'd sent him out to get a thicker skin, to learn to give and take hits, down to the part of town where people play rough. He was good with assists, but he wasn't a record-breaker who'd make it onto any computer-assembled rosters. He was elected to oblivion, he can't survive—that's the destiny of 99.9% of Swiss soccer players, if not 100%. Switzerland is not, in football, a nation of geniuses.

– True, true, Mr. Window blurted out, who at the ex-masseur's words felt like a scrambled egg, a piece of blotting paper that, if a drop of ink fell on it, would be consumed entirely.

– True, true, Scribe O/17360 hastened to add. And wait till you hear this: on March 10th, I wrote to the Servette Football Club of Geneva, and not even five days later they responded with a card that was all nice with a garnet-colored header, like the Servette jerseys. The top left corner listed their complete information: when the club was founded, when they had won the championship, the Cup, the Alpine Cup, the League Cup. The letter, in a literal translation, went like this:

Dear Sir,

We acknowledge receipt of your letter from 10 March to which we paid our utmost attention. Unfortunately, in searching our records, we found no trace of any documents concerning Mr. Walaschek in our archives. We're very sorry for this. Please trust, dear Sir, in the expression of our best sentiments.

***

General Secretary

"We found no trace": incompetents! with all their Servette laundries to erase everything, annihilate, eradicate, bleach whiter than white. Erase it all, like the tree inside Berkeley's mind (1685–1753) when his mind thinks of something other than a tree, because for Berkeley as well material objects exist only when they are perceived. *Esse est percipi.* And when a soccer player has finished being perceived by the crowds filling the stands, that player is erased from the face of the earth. Total eclipse.

A compatriot of the monumental center forward John Charles, Sir Bertrand of Wales, began to recite:

> There was a young man who said "God
> Must think it exceedingly odd
> > If he finds that this tree
> > Continues to be
> When there's no one about in the Quad."

The tree of the philosopher and bishop Berkeley was none other than Eugene Walaschek, and more than a few Swiss then showed a sudden interest in the philosophy of perception. But Sir Bertrand didn't want to cause anxiety or shock, thus he re-

sumed his recitation, responding thus, for everyone's benefit, to
the young man:

> "Dear Sir:
> Your astonishment's odd;
> *I* am always about in the Quad.
> And that's why the tree
> Will continue to be
> Since observed by,
> *Yours faithfully,*
> God."

God allowed himself a hearty laugh. Then, to demonstrate
his godly gratitude (or as Jupiter omnipotens, or *Wille*—but the
horseshoer raised a point of order: this was not the time to split
hairs, call him God and not another word!), because Walaschek
too, perceived by God, became proof of God's existence! Imperceptibly, he stirred the hand of a degenerate painter, moved him
to take a sheet of newspaper (page 13 from the April 19, 1938
National Zeitung), to take black ink, a regular brush, and paint
an O over Walaschek's name. Which in turn became proof of
God's existence, and therefore much more than the top of a well
from which one can draw water. Because there was a baker who
insisted:

– A player who quits playing is a well without a drop of water.
Done. Dry for all eternity.

Animals no longer go to that well to sate their thirst, making
those beautiful, concentric geometric waves that break gently
against its walls. An ex-soccer player becomes like an ex-bathtub,

all chipped, with big stains, rusty fixtures. And yet who knows how many beautiful women have gone and lain in that tub, running their hands over their white bellies and thighs, savoring the warm water and foam. Now the tub sits in the middle of a meadow in mid-autumn, in the November fog, once in a while someone fills it up with a garden hose . . .

Sir Bertrand of Wales, without taking his eyes off the math journal spread open on his knees, which he was reading for pleasure, once again broke the silence:

– When a player stops playing, he becomes a black hole. He becomes the trans-finite, Cantor's aleph-0 . . .

– A black hole? The baker was in a huff. Would you, please, pretty please, for ignorant old me, get your head out of the clouds and put your feet on the ground?

– My feet on the ground? My friend, you have no idea! My feet on the ground! That'd be quite a stretch. But do you or do you not realize that your Achilles-heart will never catch up to the Walaschek-tortoise? That Walaschek is, like every other common man—like you too—an infinity?

– Oh, that's a good one. That's the first time anyone's told me I'm infinite. I'll tell that to my wife, who thinks the complete opposite, the numbskull.

– And she thinks wrong, if that's what she thinks. Go ahead and tell her that Klee and Cantor's aleph-0, the limit of the infinitely small, have the same property of in-ac-cess-i-bil-i-ty as the Walaschek-infinite. Tell her . . .

The baker suggested, at supersonic speed, in the ear of the horseshoer, standing next to him, that: – If I ruled the world, I'd take that phony who's blathering on, I'd put him in my oven at three hundred degrees, and if he got cranky I'd tell him he's no philosopher of the infinite, and I'd let him bake to infinity, till he's cooked right through. Sir Bertrand gave the baker the look of a teacher keeping an eye on a troublemaker. He raised his voice just slightly:

– So I'm Cantor's aleph-0, Eugene Walaschek, insofar as we are all "objects," we are inaccessible, immeasurable? That means—finally, we've got it!—that means that Klee's O on the April 19, 1938 *National Zeitung* is a black hole, a condensed body with a gravitational field so intense that no matter, no light, can come out of it. So Walaschek the star (every man is a star, a stellar micro-mass) will remain invisible.

– Yeah, sure.

– What do you mean yeah, sure? the horseshoer cut in.

– Are people not free to call out "yeah, sure" anymore?

Sir Bertrand, seeing that the crowd wanted to push both him and philosophy offside, out of play, pointed to the math book he was reading and said:

– Yes, it's true. In other words, we're part of a grand design, too grand for us to comprehend. We can't describe it in the way that we can describe external objects or individual character, somehow isolating them from the flow, the flow of history I mean, in which their existence lies, or from their submerged, unexplored positions, to which professional historians have paid so little attention.

The horseshoer tried to stifle a flow of laughter and tears. Into the baker's right ear, he decanted:

– Make good and sure you don't say anything to your wife or anyone else in your coop, but we're smack in the middle of a zoo. Or the looney bin, if you prefer.

Sir Bertrand didn't notice the interruption.

– There exists a magic circle into which no measurement can take us. As such, for a modern scientist, it is a "unicum" of geometry. That is, space and time. You could, like an astronaut, explore the inside of a black hole, but you wouldn't be able to come back to report what you saw. All hope of return dashed: it's like that obscure writing over the gates of hell: Abandon all hope . . . Will you be abandoned to cry in the blackness of that night? Or will you float on the waves of space in a sweet delirium?

What if, instead of a black hole, it was a halo? It was a halo! Why couldn't a man like Walaschek, in his individualistic individuality—monastic, monos, mono—why couldn't he have been taken up to the sky in a beam of light?

– Yes, yes, interjected a member of the Society of Jesus by the name of Père Jean-Pierre. – In abandon, the only rule is the present moment; and the soul is as light as a feather, fluid as water, simple as a little boy; it's as mobile as a ball in receiving and following all the impulses of grace. Souls like this are no more consistent or rigid than cast metal; and just as metal takes the form of the mold into which it is poured, these souls bend and adapt with equal facility to all the forms that God wants to give them; in a word, their pliability resembles that of air, which yields to every puff of wind, and assumes any shape.

– All we needed was a priest, grumbled Snoozy, opening his left eye a crack, and taking advantage of this subliminal jolt to take a big swig of beer. All we needed was a priest. *Nuntio vobis gaudium magnum*: the gap has been filled. The priest is here. The priest hath spoken. Priests are like parsley, like potato beetles, like robinia, they invade every wasteland.

A priest used to listening to all sorts of confessions wouldn't let himself be bothered by crap from some ignorant ass. His badger eyes lighting up in his big plump face, he said:

– Have you, Mr. Walaschek, experienced ecstasy?

– Ecstasy? Ecstasy is floating in air. I've known lots who are better than I, a Brit, for example, Robinson, I believe. Our Gyger. Gyger paired up with the giant Steffen, and they made a good barrier, much better than the Maginot line. Once I saw Gyger make a play that was a marvel. There was a high ball coming from far away, a long pass for the center forward. Gyger sprang for it immediately and jumped up for a head butt. And everyone stood there motionless, because everyone, even we Swiss, I as well as the others, thought Gyger's timing was off, way too early. But Gyger kept going up, then he contracted his Germanic—not German—muscles a little, then he stayed in the air like that for an endless moment, and I thought his eyes were going to pop out of his head, and then his tan head hit the ball straight on with a dull thud. He looked like a Greek bronze hanging on an invisible string. But who remembers Gyger now?

– He had Germanic muscles? Simone Weil jumped in, not in ecstasy, just conquering her acute shyness—she who loved the discipline and will of the Germanics as much as she hated the arrogance of the Hitlerites, the Napoleons, sun kings, the abhorred Romans.

– I said Germanic just because, I could have used another word. Minelli had Germanic muscles too, without belonging to the German race.

– If I understand right, chimed Mr. Window, in the tone of a teacher trying hard to make his students laugh, that also means

72

that if he'd charged at me one hundred percent, Gyger would have obliterated me?

– Like a Jew.

– Bless you! the teacher said.

– Oh, what an irreparable loss for the Wind Factories that would be!

They all turned toward the back: it was the voice of Asshat—that's what they called him, because on top of his reddish hair he always wore a military wedge cap. And since everyone's eyes were on him, on his baker's face, he was emboldened and said:

– Mr. Klee's O is nothing but a donut, a donut with a hole, the ones that ugly brute Herr Göring liked and also that Countess Cack up my cul-de-sac who refuses to look me in the face. Hitler, on the other hand, liked cookies. Because Hitler was someone, if you'll allow me to use a peasant term, was someone who was raised on *angrùan*, that is, rose hips, which tighten you up (because that's how you say tighten in Latin, my Latin teacher explained it to me), they tighten you up in the rear just like they do in the mouth; with types like Hitler the bottom and the top are the same thing, that's why Hitler barked with his mouth contorted under that ugly moustache. For him, talking must have been like it is for someone who's constitutionally constipated to take a shit: he has to strain every muscle in his ass.

But the others, forming a semi-circle, seemed to say, and actually one of them did say: – Now instead of the Doctors of the Church we have to listen to bakers? So me, a truck driver, I can get up and say my two cents as a truck driver, and go on and on longer than the number of miles I've put on my truck going down all the roads of Europe lain end to end.

In short, what happened was that—as happens in all the public assemblies in the world—at first nobody says a word, but if you do the slightest thing to encourage them to talk, and finally you find the one who, just to get it over with, says he'll break the ice, then it's all over: too much confidence leads to the loss of reverence. The truck driver rose to his feet and looked around the room as if he were the Duce's right hand. He was the antipodes of someone like the man from Fontana, smart and humble, who said to his next-door neighbor as he was going out with a length of twine: Don't get excited now—even if I've traveled the world I've always just been making bales of hay.

So projecting his voice from his stomach like an understudy of the Duce, the truck driver posited, no doubt about it, that Mr. Klee's O was one of those circles—*cercini*—that women in the south put on their heads to carry jars—that's why their backs are as straight as wires. – And once I saw a player called Lempen who seemed like he had one of those circles right on his forehead . . .

But the truck driver, seeing that they were all turned toward him, with their ears perked up like jackrabbits', felt his gab motor switch off, as if his battery had suddenly drained, so he looked pleadingly at his daughter's geography teacher. Who, like a good teacher, understood immediately and didn't make him say it twice.

– Yes, I know. I remember that young man Lempen very well. Once he stopped the ball with his head, in mid-field, and the ball stayed there, like a magnet, because the way Lempen's nose met his forehead, it formed a nice little basin, a little *foppa*, as the shepherds in our Alps say, that matched the curve of the ball perfectly.

The Arctic of the ball fit into the vault of Lempen's sky. Lempen ran in long strides, solemn, aristocratic, with that ball magnetized onto his head, toward the opponent's goal. At sixteen meters, what did he do? He stopped, jerked his frontal Antarctica and like a world-weary Atlas, let the world roll down his thigh to his instep, setting up a hopeless shot, casting the world into the void: straight into the net.

There was a—though in truth, slightly timid—round of applause for Lempen, but without detracting from Lempen's good, great, immense merits, the thin baker decanted one of his deepest skepticisms into the fat baker's right ear:

– These guys are crazy: black holes, jar-bearers. Fit to be tied. There are too many philosophers around nowadays and philosophers are the sort who are capable of going to the osteria and instead of ordering an omelette they demand a plate of philosophy. And if the waitress brings them a big frothy mug of horse piss instead of a beer, they drink the horse piss and think it's their Carlsberg. And with all their persistence in believing for belief's sake, they'd even get themselves killed without batting an eye. Or put on the grill to roast like a spare rib. In the Sicilian bull down in Agrigento. Steer clear.

Out loud, vehemently, a colleague of the geography teacher's jumped in. A history teacher.

– Why is it that in this country, which began in long-ago 1291, a country completely shorn of its memories, why is it that nobody talks about Lempen, Walaschek, Vonlanthen, anymore? Try asking the first kid who passes by. He'll look at you like someone on insulin shock treatments. Vonlanthen played in Italy, and the

Italians, constitutionally incapable of pronouncing a foreign name correctly, called him Volante. *Der fliegende Schweizer*, the flying Swissman. He wasn't a pure sprinter, but he had a long stride, and at the first game he played—in Genoa, the Italian Academy of Soccer (in the stands, mixed with the plebs, were the Peripatetics of soccer, Aristotle and all the Alcibiadeses of the stadiums)—everyone proclaimed, with a broad consensus, that few trotting halfbacks could have competed with Volante's loping stride when it was worthily executed.

Walaschek closed his half-closed eyes even more. He dreamed.

Pulver

Alcibiades   Hannibal

Lempen   Socrates   Aristotle

Plotinus   Walaschek   Plato   Vonlanthen   Sulla

– Why Sulla? the history teacher shot forth, like a viper. He was completely and totally like Stalin. With his proscriptions! Of course, Sulla didn't have the messengers Stalin did, with his "technology," which allowed him to send his carrier pigeon all the way to Mexico to bash Trotsky's brains in! Thus striking fear into everyone, because everyone felt like they were reachable—and they were—in any part of the world. By the Great Purger, there in Moscow.

– Why Sulla? It's a nice name, fast, for a winger. Like Gento, which rhymes with *vento*, wind. A guy from Bellinzona, seeing him on TV, said: To buy him from Real Madrid we'd have to sell at least one of our castles.

– If you took a poll, half the city would have been for it. Bellinzona has three castles, after all—there'd still be two left.

But now, pretty much everyone, spurred on by the two bakers and the truck driver who was putting on airs like some sort of jet-setter, everyone wanted to jump in with an opinion, democratically requesting (are we or are we not in Switzerland?) a turn.

For starters, no less boldly than a father of the bride who plants himself in the center of all seventy guests for the commemorative photograph, Mr. Pearlsbeforeswine (this was the secret nickname his neighbors had given him, and it had spread throughout the neighborhood), a retired sergeant major, said:

– Ladies, gentlemen: to me, that circle—if it is a circle, which is something yet to be proven—can have only one meaning: it's the bowl for the Kappel War milk soup. In Zwingli's time, Swiss Catholics and Swiss Protestants—O woe, woe, woe!—were battling each other. But in the end, the Swiss spirit prevailed over differences in faith. The Catholic leaders and the Protestant leaders gathered around a big pot filled with bread and milk and ate this soup together on the border between the cantons of Zürich and Zug. Anyone who reached past his side received a friendly hand-slap with the spoon. They were wooden spoons. Thus in 1938, on April 18 at the Wankdorf, thus every day, from Geneva to Buochs, Basel to Chiasso: instead of the pot, the cup; instead of the soup, a cheery wine. From the Swiss Cup drink the captain of the winning team, the federal councilor, authorities, and managers, the winning team, the losers. Every region in the country, every valley, the nation's villages, its cities, joined in the diversity of languages and faiths—they drink, metaphorically, from the Cup.

One and all gather 'round the flag.
Red is the flame that burns in our hearts,

White the smile that noble fervor imparts.
If ever one day we see it from us be lift,
For the white, for the red, we shall raise our fist.

They drank red and white. Walaschek, who in that very year, 1938, had endless troubles acquiring a Swiss passport, closed his laughing eyes at the abundance of names that came gushing out:

Tell

Euler   Oecolampadius

Lavater   Winkelried   Stauffacher

Gotthelf   Calvin   Zwingli   Walaschek   Keller

Jung

Paracelsus   Gessner

Hodler   Bachofen   Vadian

Koblet   Walaschek   Ramuz   Grock   Constant

A bit overwhelming, the German presence in the first formation. The Italian-language newspapers would have made a fuss. They always do. The same old vexations of those *Vögte*, reeves, on the other side of the Alps. The leopard may change its spots, but . . . And Francesco Chiesa once gave a botanical-moralistic speech saying that the Swiss, by trampling the Italian flower that grew in the Swiss garden, were damaging their own garden. They should have given Chiesa the Grand Schiller Prize a second and third time. In the second half, they could bring in Borromini and Serodine, Swiss who, moreover, were a little suspect, corrected or corrupted as they were by the Roman air. And Major Davel? They might have blamed the Vaudese. And Werner Stauffacher, Hans Waldmann, Le Corbusier, Cendrars, Giacometti, Spitteler, the two Burckhardts. On the bench, Scartazzini and Orelli (Johann Caspar), but, my dear sons, there are only eleven spots, and a center halfback like Winkelried ("By gathering with a wide embrace, / Into his single heart, / a sheaf of fatal Austrian spears."), you certainly can't leave him out. More grace than we asked for, St. Anthony!

– *La grz'ia t' st'Ntonio è 'n la brca t' furbol!*

St. Anthony's grace is part of the business of football, or "furbol," as the butcher put it, who had garbled his words a little trying to speak standard Italian. Thus he made a frantic phone call direct to the ear of the pharmacist, who, with the meticulousness of a man meting out poison, meticulously translated:

– Mr. Painter! May this perchance be a ring that his lordship painted on humble paper, a rigid round chain—one of the rings of which the so-called sporting organizations avail themselves to catch and bind innocent youths, bind their hands and feet?

The pharmacist stood up, walked over to the table where there was a small bottle of the produce of some national spring—he wanted to water his mouth before spouting other locutionary flowers. But he didn't take into account the journalists present, and one of those paper-staining phonies saw that it was the ideal moment to nip that latinorum in the bud. He rushed to speak, trying to flatter the noble pharmacist at the same time:

– It's true, it's true. As the man of science said so well, they catch them by the thousands. They have a whole web and where the strands meet they plant their local referees, the coaches of little teams, the fan clubs who root out a susceptible kid as soon as that kid dribbles the ball à la Schiaffino, so to speak, or *parva si licet*, a shot à la Mortensen. He's got the stuff, he has talent. And they buy these guys for nothing. I mean, they give the kid, instead of a contract, they give him a nice spot at the academy, they bring him up as if in Sparta—logical analysis in the morning and kicks in the shins after lunch, crosswords in the evening and then early to bed. When it's the right time they'll throw him in with the Juniors 4, then 3, then 2, then 1, then with Hopefuls B, Hopefuls A, and if he has any talent, fifteen minutes on the top team, if the top team is already up three to zero. Billiards and Scala Quaranta at night, hearty slaps on the back, snickering, jealousy, secrets. If his debut on the top team goes well, his ranking will shoot up. They'll send him out on loan, or open him up to shared ownership, or sell him outright to some provincial team.

The butcher who was mangling his words in that speech about boys bought and sold like prostitutes, call girls, women to be trafficked, switched on his mental computer and from this computer it came out that, all things considered, he treated his little pigs no worse when he tied a rope around their legs and tied the rope to one of the rings at the butcher shop; and if he could give his piglets some advice, it would be: relax, don't move, don't yell, you're not going anywhere anyway.

The diabolical Klee, however, thought: if sports really have a certain fascist connotation, does that mean that there's something good about fascism? Or is that an enthymeme? Life is full of enthymemes, of cherry-rationales with worms inside them. And when a "Johnny of the Vine, who sometimes smiles and sometimes cries," a Gianni Rivera for example, who gets onto his first team at sixteen, gets to pair up with Schiaffino—does he or doesn't he pay the expenses for a thousand boys and ten academies? The expense! But back at home, when they find out that Gianni is playing on the top team, the entire family, the entire community, the entire territory—the nation, from the provosts lined up for the big Mass to the altar boys who convert to the boys' team. The stadiums fill up when they win, it's true. But everything is built on the faith of the faithful, especially in a period of crisis, which sooner or later comes for everyone.

The nation and the world, the universe: from Ambrose's old Ambrosiana to Internazionale, from Internazionale Milano to Inter Milan. It's not Bern, the city with the Wankdorf, where Eugene Walaschek played, but "Young Boys." In Basel the "Old Boys" stay young and in Zurich it's the "Young Fellows" and the "Blue Stars" or "Red Stars." Many towns forget themselves—or dream? (for all of life is a dream, and dreams, after all, are dreams)—and call their teams Racing, Dinamo, Rapid, Urania. Juventus is a name beyond the city, both beneath and beyond the nation.

Klee laughed openly with a truly degenerate laugh. But Klee—if you'll pardon the insinuation—what did Klee know about Sindelar, whom the sports writers called "Der Papierene," the Paper Man, for his slender grace and dexterity and adroitness and feline dribbling skill, but who was actually tissue paper in the face of a Nazi tank? If only he had the bulk of a Plánička, the great Czech cat, shrewd, massive, spry, the only one who was able to succeed Zamora as all-star goalie. No, paper—burned by gas.

81

Suddenly, a wind came that shook all the leaves off all of Klee's trees, and all the birds hidden in the leaves flew off, half-carried by the wind.

– It's not so funny, said Lodovico, the chub fisherman. He had a grandson who, ever since they'd put him with the "young talents," it was like he'd been brainwashed.

– He won't even say hi to me anymore, that says it all!

No, that didn't say it all; all eyes were on the fisherman, waiting for something else.

And so the good Lodovico of the chubs slowly added some things:

– To me, Mr. Klee's O is the circle that they cut in the ice, when the Balaton, or all those lakes like the Balaton, freeze, and when they're frozen like that they put a light over the hole and all the fish rush over, and they're all there for the taking, hundreds of pounds' worth, you can sell 'em to all of Europe and still keep a glut for yourself. It's a kind of fishing I don't like. It's not a sport, at least not in the way I think of sport. But that's what almost all those glutton tycoons do, at least ninety percent of them, just like the tycoons of oil or construction or whatever other tomfoolery, they seem like philanthropists but they play the devil's game. They know they can wring their workers like rags. They know that when they've squeezed everything out of them they can just get rid of them. They know there's a thick cement that binds them, the schmucks, a drug that placates them and puts them to sleep—it's sports, the home team, the Big Family of Sports. They squeeze fans and players like lemons, and anyone who can't take it gets thrown into Gehenna.

Lodovico, the chub fisherman, spoke with increasing difficulty, as if he had dough in his mouth or were still recovering from his second heart attack. He made a gesture as if tossing aside, albeit gently, a deck of cards—I'm done playing.

Due to professional instruction and destruction, Mr. Window, who couldn't stand the prolonged silences in the inquiry, bestowed upon them a few kernels of poetry.

– Like the sorceress Alcina, you mean, in Ariosto:

> Alcina drew the fishes to the shore,
> With nought but simple words and magic power.

But it's difficult to interrupt a teacher who sees the world as a classroom. Luckily, the bank teller said:

– Klee's O isn't Giotto's O—this is an indisputable fact. His O is merely a letter of the alphabet, and I think that in all our talk we seem to have forgotten that the work is called *Alphabet I*. As far as the O, perhaps precisely because of its position in the alphabet, and in the painting it's next to H, to P, it forms the cheer from 1938: *Hop Suisse, hop Walaschek, hop* what? Hop old tired Europa, tempted by the lusty bull god who tempts the old ones too, the Moloch who can't be eliminated from the face of the earth, from the heart of the individual? But Klee's O looks quite like one of Saturn's rings, or, better yet, coral, limey and hard, arboreal, of a color varying from pinkish white to red, composed of the skeletons . . .

Christ, listening to all this crap made Vincent want to cut off his other ear:

– But tell me, he pleaded, under his breath, black and white, can we use them or not, are they perhaps forbidden fruit?

– Sssssh, Mr. Window is talking, someone in the second-to-last row said. He's my daughter's teacher, he's excellent.

– If you'd let me talk, Mr. Window said roundly. That's not exactly what I meant: I meant that the O over the name of, what's his name, Walaschek, is a navel, it's the link to our primal nourishment, to memory. But your sports, on the other hand—what is it connected to that lasts? Your sports is the moment, it's the ephemeral, it's oblivion. What does it leave behind, like a trail of snail slime, besides a few statistics, trophies, press reports like the one in the April 19th *National Zeitung*: a trivial heap of petty talk. It's the herbarium, the museum of the banal, it's death. Klee wanted to paint death.

– Bravo, well said, cried out the man who'd had the two heart attacks. Others, however, kept yapping, like untrained puppies.

– Doesn't he speak like a poet? said the man in the second-to-last row to his left-hand neighbor. The orator-teacher waved his hands downwards to request patience and order.

– If I were the curator of an exhibit of the work of the esteemed painter Paul Klee, I would put his crimson Creator high up, in the center, like Michelangelo's Christ in the Sistine Chapel. He too comes down from the sky, all bulky and muscular yet with the appearance of a squat sparrowhawk that has just flown a little ways away to spend a moment contemplating what he has created . . .

– By the hundreds, the thousands! exclaimed a young art history scholar, who still wore braids and looked like a little girl—who knows how she would have been able to control a classroom full of rowdy kids. He made cats with yarn, she said, dogs-with-without-leashes, angels, housewives, people about town, masks, fights, wonders, floating cities and flags without swastikas, flags of no nation, just to make children happy the world over and adults too, who have a bit of the child they once were conserved inside themselves: everyone who loves to be made happy by the beauties of creation—little girls too, of course, lots of them, and women . . .

Van Gogh, his head bowed, was perhaps thinking about the potential of an osteria's shadows. But at the word "women" it was no longer possible to restrain the red-bearded painter with the missing ear. Turning to his brother Theo, he said:

– It is the same everywhere, in the country as much as in the city—one has to take women into account if one wants to be up to date. If I paint peasant women I want them to be peasant women—so I want to get a whore's expression when I paint whores. That is precisely why a whore's head by Rembrandt struck me so forcefully. Because he had caught that mysterious smile in such an infinitely beautiful way, with a gravity of his very own—the magician of magicians. This is something new for me, and I want to achieve it at all costs. Manet has done it and Courbet—well, *sacrebleu*, I've the same ambition too, the more so as I've felt the infinite beauty of the study of women . . .

Is there a woman behind every soldier? How many behind a soccer player? We shouldn't completely rule out the possibility that one half of Walaschek (the top half?) was dead even before Klee divided him with his O in April 1938. One evening in autumn, or winter, they had gotten back to Geneva late after a brutal game in the rain, too late to catch a bus home, so the coach, who was gruff as always but incapable of leaving a kid in the lurch, proposed to his inside forward, that promising boy with the eastern name, that he stay at his place. Two minutes to set up the sofa, no big deal. A young man can even sleep on the floor. Even the coach could have slept on the floor. At the end of the game they—players and managers—had nearly come to blows. Now the sleep of good health. After having a bite to eat, drumming his fingers a little on the oilcloth and remembering that useless bastard referee, chaos in midfield, he slowly sipped his last glass: don't take the pearls away from the swine, he had picked up and left without ceremony, thank you and good night. For eight hours he wouldn't be available to anyone. Meanwhile, the coach's daughter had prepared the makeshift bed as well as some compresses for the blow Walaschek had taken straight on. The black hole comes later. A man's life, and a woman's life even more so, is full of black holes. Years later, that's when a wind rushes through that rustles all the leaves in the tree of memory, and the birds who sought refuge from the hurricane fly far away as if four thousand hunters had arrived with rifles aimed. What words, what gazes, what gestures, what father-coach is there between the coach's daughter and this kid who needs a compress? From nowhere in her throat could the coach's daughter find a saint's simple words to say: You called, you shouted, you shattered my deafness!

Why are many young women, barely more than girls, led to consider, like the coach's daughter, the Sunday alternative as the only alternative? Why didn't that young half-winger inside forward take flight and swoop her out of the paternal tempest, take her away from the unhealthy desire—on a spiteful impulse—for tranquility? What to add? Is there anything to add? That love, as one of the Church Fathers says, is only an "accident in substance"?

But a coach doesn't know, and nobody puts the blame on him, neither Church Fathers nor Roman ones. He's busy with coaching, that's all.

Could one conjecture that Walaschek hadn't read as assiduously as he should have in the book-of-hours-eyes of the coach's daughter? One could. Without placing a hint of blame on him. If he is guilty, it's only of being young, and tired, and naïve. His eyes were slightly rimmed with red—a little bunny, a pink ermine, a baby bird outside its nest. Did he perhaps have a touch of fever? Dear dear boy!

And as he waited for the thermometer reading (in his groin!), Walaschek, like a gawky confirmand, his head with its little tuft of hair, tried to break away: no, Miss, he was fine, really, he didn't want to be a bother, it was embarrassing, she was doing too, too much for someone like him . . .

In the '30s, if someone had taken a poll—though at that time they weren't yet in vogue, ecumenical sociology was still in its infancy—it would have unequivocally shown that the majority of the Swiss people, much as they had persisted in the use of the Swiss dialect over "proper" German from Germany, had likewise upheld the tradition of placing thermometers under the armpit, the left, and not in the groin or the mouth. Therefore, as she waited, serious, for the mercury to respond, something happened inside the coach's daughter: the coach's daughter saw, telepathically—"like in a dream," she would have said—her cousin Silvia of Silenen, who was her spitting image. Of their two fathers—brothers—one had gone to work for the railroad (now on the verge of retirement, in Silenen), the other was a storekeeper for department stores and also a coach. A coach's daughter may come to find herself surrounded by straight- or knock-kneed boys almost always sore with bruises, like seedlings in a lovely field trampled and poked at by a herd of hogs, in the same way that Silvia of Silenen, the daughter of Silenen's stationmaster, living right above the two station offices, says the air she breathes in that "heart of Switzerland" is nothing but the air of a waiting room, and her eyes and ears are completely filled with trains heading north and south, to the ends of the world. If she opens her eyes, her eyes fall on the station name, Silenen—it's the sign that, at night, white and blue, bangs against her eyelids.

But one day, she'd get on a train and . . .

And who knows where she ended up, well beyond Arth-Goldau, Olten. One lazy day, already distant in the memory of her cousin from Geneva, Silvia of Silenen stood with parted legs on a little street near the station, already in open countryside; making a perfect isosceles triangle, holding her dainty little blonde head high, in a pose that would have made even St. Bonaventure's blood tingle, so frenzied was he at the triangle formed by the trinity that he saw triangles everywhere—and then Klee, all catlike and triangular too, smiles, because he could have drawn in three strokes the girl's supreme oracular triangle, with a circle at each of the three points: A, head; B, left foot; C, right foot, let's go ahead and call these circles little Os (every one a little Klee O), and in each of those three circles put the three forces that press upon man and also, and violently, on that slender plume called Silvia of Silenen: greed, lust for domination, sex; and then, by each one, three little cherry-balls (as Klee goes on drawing and painting a sprig of mistletoe with its cluster of little berries and a web of covalent branch-segments holding them together). One could add other berries, other ganglia, other nuclei, other atoms in a dense molecule—from sex, for example, comes ferocity, masochism, a "spiteful impulse" for escape, and Sade; sublimated into the army, the stadiums, the desire to conceive a child, and a hundred other desires, ad infinitum. From the sprig of berries of the *libido dominandi* mistletoe, Klee could have deduced—for himself, for his art—another sub-triangle, with three distinct points, as an attempt at sovereign domination, through the act of creation, over the interaction of Physis (his Greco-Roman heritage), Psyche (Christian introspection, Augustine's cornerstone: his metaphysics in first person, in the vocative), and the eye of his I: Klee's.

Silvia of Silenen had not placed philosophy in any of the three points of her triangle, but rather what she saw, in her colorless eighteen years of life (a diagnosis that looked like a facsimile of the appraisal her cousin from Geneva, the coach's daughter, might have given herself, in her colorless twenty-six years of life). She put: 1) that a father is almost always a constraining constraint, the Old Testament against the New; 2) he's someone who sometimes treats his daughter's heart like a blacksmith treats a mare's hoof that needs to be reshod, or acts like an underpaid boy who reciprocates his meager pay with a sideways kick to the belly-sac of the she-goat suffering from scabies on her udders just because she'd made him spill a full pail of milk; and 3) (though the third was said more with Silvia's fair hands than with words, thus Scribe O/17360 has decreed with his cloddish paw):

a father considers it normal for there to be one person with the only right to speak (him), against another who's all body (the daughter), fragile, soft, and earthy, filled with urges, feelings, fits of anger. For example: for Silvia of Silenen, who knows? For the coach's daughter: a young man, that boy with the thermometer in his groin, with the foreign name, who plays soccer—she can feel it—like a god.

Something happened to the coach's daughter, something similar to what happened to Virginia of Ronco, who would stand at the window of her osteria every day in winter watching the snow fall, the expanse of white: Bedoleto buried in snow, La Villa buried in snow, Ossasco buried in snow (and perhaps Eliseo was staring at his glass without thinking of the snow because when he was concentrating he didn't like to be distracted) and La Fontana buried in the snow (and maybe Franku 't Zan; idem for Eliseo)— and the world, for Virginia, with her white, thin hair, could be concentrated and reduced to Eliseo and Franku 't Zan, to their two glasses, but then one April day, Virginia, parting the curtains, saw two people coming down the path dug out of the snow and called out excitedly: – So many people in the world, and here's two more coming to Le Sacche, because for Virginia at least half the world was concentrated in those two walking through the snow: and so it was for the coach's daughter, a virgin of overripe virginity, twenty-six!, for whom humanity came down to:

a coach/father;

a boy who must be the inside forward: Walaschek . . .

And because he's one of the hundred thousand fathers who can be terrible fathers, the coach's daughter won't even wait to hear his hand on the handle, the door opening, the words old as the Old Testament: I have to talk to you . . .

So the coach's daughter will embark on a short long journey. Not having been able to choose the day she was born, she would choose the day she'll die. *Ite missa est.*

No one having intervened to lift a finger in defense of fathers, Walaschek, years later, lowered his eyelids further. One thing is certain: years later, he doesn't like to talk about women. He won't answer questions of that sort. What does all this stuff about painters or women have to do with soccer anyway? In vain, a few journalists had tried to get him to talk (and immediately—as was to be expected—Nietzsche and Schopenhauer started (and not quietly) hurling insults at those vermin of society that are journalists), asking what they had done in Paris between the two games against Hitler's Germany, and if they'd celebrated their victory, if they'd gone to a club, if, if: because someone said, later, that they were a little wobbly during the game against the Hungarians.

"What about women?" Nothing. Silence. Fortunately, just like in life, a minute of silence lasts much less than a minute. Fortunately, everyone's attention was already directed elsewhere, due to a jokester who, jeering and making everyone laugh (Walaschek opened his right eye halfway), joined his thumbs and index fingers, to form, approximately, a circle, an oval.

– Pshaw, O, oval. Signore e signori, meine Damen und Herren, Mesdames, Messieurs, don't be offended, don't take this the wrong way, I'm not coming from left field (I'm not a leftist, anyway) but that thing that was painted over the glorious name of Eugene Walaschek is something else altogether. It's the ass of Switzerland, or should I say sphincter? In 1938, the Milanese, both in and out of the Arena, said it was luck when our boys sent Portugal packing. Bare-assed luck, post/crossbar hits, and also Huber, the goalie for the national team, who had every St. Nicholas on his side. Same with England, and, frankly, with Germany too. Switzerland is the most lucky-ass country in the world. Everyone gives us shit for it, in fact. But why aren't they more like us, those fools? We live in peace. We have for centuries. The Federal Council, luck or no, could forget all about us and pop open a bottle of champagne. And if the nationals were the emblem, the paradigm of the military, Herr Hitler would have to think twice before attacking us. Careful, barber, that's my face you're shaving. Don't touch the high tension wires. We're not the Maginot line. We don't have leaders with names like Daladier, Gamelin, Chamberlain, names like . . . Gamelin's like a scullery boy's name. And Pétain . . .

But now, following that joker, everyone was all excited to guess what the O, that mysterious object, could be, as if they were on a game show (everyone except for Vincent, who kept on talking, privately, to Theo, maybe thinking about jerseys for the ideal women's team? "Anyway," he was saying, "the color range: a flesh color full of tonal values, with more bronze on the neck, jet-black hair—black which I had to do with carmine and Prussian blue—off-white for the little jacket, light yellow, much lighter than the white, for the background. A touch of flame red in the jet-black hair and again a flame-colored bow in the off-white. She's a girl from a café chantant and yet the expression I was looking for was somewhat 'ecce homo-like'")—in short, they were all trying to guess. Like on the radio when they play a strange noise and people can call in to guess what it is, and whoever gets it right wins a prize. In 1938, even before April 18, before the Servette-Grasshoppers game at the Wankdorf, they could have recorded the sounds of strange instruments and devices and gadgets in Dachau, Auschwitz, Buchenwald, *und so weiter*, then broadcast them on the radio and no one—even if they perked up on their couch or their chair trying to concentrate so that they could hazard a guess—would have gotten it right. Of course, if they rang the bells of Vienna, all of them, as they did at dusk on March 14 (it was, pardon the insistence and perhaps slightly German pedantry, 1938) to welcome, "amidst the jubilation of the crowd, Chancellor Hitler, direct from Schönbrunn," well that's easy, everyone knows that sound: bells. But if they're bone-breaking, muscle-flattening devices, tools that strip skin down to the bicep, testicle-removers, extractors for nails or teeth or fillings, brass knuckles on the eyebulb or the heart or the solar plexus, expandable devices that stretch beyond measure (a foot and a half? much more than Procustes) delicate parts to be beaten crossways with dull blows of the baton, ox-whips, sacks of sand like punching bags, against the lower belly, *und so weiter*, no demagogy here—to decode them (but this is third-hand conjecture, purely academic, because they'd never broadcast such sounds, only marches, and "Lili Marleen," and bells, even *Lohengrin* too, and whoever guesses right wins!) it would take the scientists from Mauthausen, *und so weiter*. To avoid misunderstanding, let us repeat: the game is easy, and whoever's lucky enough to win will win and take home his nice gold napoleons.

– It's the ring of the Nibelungen, one of them ventured.

– It's the O of *Das Rhinegold*, another said.

– The O of Lorelei, said a third.

– Bah! Rhine gold! the geography teacher gesticulated, all in a huff. The Rhine is Swiss, too. It's pure snow water, at least up to Basel-Kleinhüningen. After that, he said smugly, I couldn't say.

– There's no gold in the Rhine, it's in the banks. Is there silver in the Aar? Nonsense. In Lugano, some of the waste from the shore drains into the Tresa, which goes from Lake Lugano to Lago Maggiore and then to the Ticino and the Po. But who can make out the water from the Ticino in the water of the Po? It's one big family. Everything goes down into the Adriatic, forming a nice fertile delta or a reed thicket full of mosquitoes, billions and billions of mosquitoes. Mussolini can't drain everything—he already drained the Pontine Marshes . . .

No, it wasn't Rhine gold. Other contestants could try their luck.

Was it a city block? A neighborhood, a circle of shade into which the champion, all the champions, could retreat? Throw in the towel, as they say. Your bike. Your cleats.

Matthias Sindelar had gone one step further. A genius center forward, a weightless body, he turned on the gas. People said he was also distraught over his wife's death. Over Austria's death? The Wunderteam's? Sepp Herberger chose nine Austrians, making Hitler's Germany even more star-studded, but Sindelar never played against those provincials from Switzerland with their heathen dialect. Where would they bury Sindelar? Either they gave him a worthy funeral or else they treated him like a used tissue—secretly pulling it from a pocket, crumpling it up, and dropping it into the river—and the beautiful Danube, which ran every color but blue (after March 1938), would have carried it, without difficulty, without a ripple, toward the East, the Balkans, the Black Sea. Farewell.

Farewell, Black Sea, farewell black well. Black hole—not that of the physicists'—the toilet. *Chi ha paura dell'uomo nero?* Our fathers used pans with black holes to roast chestnuts. In France, where they would emigrate in the winter, one of our own, a Swiss chestnut seller, found his cart half-destroyed because he looked Jewish, and so the Swiss chestnut seller gave the offending Nazi a wallop that would have killed a calf, nearly sending him to his Moloch-god, and the French judge, after carefully considering the case, declared "c'est juste et raisonnable"; and when he came back from France, he seemed not to want to die anymore because every day he would go around telling everyone—people he knew, people he didn't, at the osteria, on the street, in the kitchen where women were still heating the coffee or pouring a glass—the story of that judge, and it always ended with "juste et raisonnable" so now everybody called him *juste-et-raisonnable*. Even the priest had stopped to listen (the nights in June were long and hot, and between the rows of grapevines and in the fenced gardens, between all the houses, there was a slow procession of fireflies) the first time—without his stocking cap, with his crew cut and curious little eyes, because even a priest has the right to hear a few curiosities besides what women reveal in the confessional. But even he, the third time he heard it, felt like laughing, saying to himself (forestalling, as they say in fùtbol, his opponent) but yes, yes, *c'est juste et raisonnable*, I can even translate it into Latin for you: *dignum et justum est, aequum et salutare*. Whereas those who translated it into dialect translated it as: *bambo*, fool, someone to be sent to the nut house. Or, before the asylums, fit to be tied, in the attic, with a nice big chain on his foot, to be brought bowls of soup as one does with stray dogs or criminals.

Klee listened to everything and was silent because it seemed impossible to him that the dictionary of 1938 still contained the words *juste et raisonnable*. Klee's eyes were like horizontal slits, gashes, the eyes of a cat who seems about to fall asleep but could pounce at any moment, whereas the eyes of the priest were little squirrel eyes.

They went on guessing.

– It's the shield, the clipeus, as the Romans called it, of the Confederates against Hitler. We won't let ourselves be eaten in fifteen minutes, like a sandwich, like Austria—we won't be bratwurst.

> We'll make you a wall
> of indomitable breasts.
> It is sweet, Helvetia,
> to die for you.

The guessing game dragged on a little and began to veer into dangerous territory. Was Klee's O the mouth of a plastic doll, like the ones in sex-shop windows surrounded by all those leather goods and studs sado-nazis are so fond of? Their mouths never close, day or night. No flies can get into a closed mouth. Or was the O one of those bone-shaped cookies, or even a bone from a body? Sir, would you like a roasted marrowbone?

They came up with other possibilities—not one, but a hundred. Among the more original was that it was the halo of a saint, of one of the Church Fathers, one of those halos rotating at supersonic speed (yet seeming stationary) above the nice bald heads of those doctors of theology featured in frescoes and icons. These are the saints in adoration, in ecstasy, reveling in holy bliss, floating in mid-air, dizzying: like in Monday's photograph of the center forward floating in mid-air, aloft, an instant before the spark, when with a dull snap of the vertebral column his neck would trigger the convulsive torsion of his head and impress rotational force onto the levitating ball, shooting it into the top corner of the net.

Behind the halo, the Great Doctors team:

Thomas

Bonaventure   Albert (the Great)

Jerome   Gregory (the Great)   Ambrose

Cyprian   Anselm of Canterbury Tertullian Walaschek William of Ockham

With a defense like that, Walaschek laughed in his dream, it'd be a cinch, even against the Red Devils. And on the bench we've got Hugh and Richard of Saint Victor, from the Anglo school. The Devils, though, they've got their strategy down pat. They'll put Cerberus at the goal of course, but otherwise, Lucifer put together a trick formation:

Malacoda

Cagnazzo   Graffiacane

Ciriatto   Alichino   Calcabrina

Draghignazzo   Rubicante   Belfagor   Beelzebub   Barbariccia

With a hothead like Libicocco on the bench? Leave it to the Devils! And Screwtape too? Worse than trying to find your goats in the middle of the woods . . . worse than a house full of women.

97

But one of the other disputants cut this short, someone they didn't know, who jumped to his feet and said:

– You blind fools, don't you realize that Klee's O is just an O? It's not a zero—it has nothing to do with omega, death, endings. Let me explain. Sit down. He had them all sit on the lawn as if he were Christ about to perform the multiplication of the loaves and the fishes; he took pity on them.

– Let me explain to you how it is. It's like closing your eyes for the last time: night falls over you, and it's even darker than a night in an alpine pass when the blizzard winds blow and you can't see more than a meter past your nose, and it's a long night, an hour of that kind of night is longer than a summer day for a man hunched over slaving under the gaping sun.

You won't be anything anymore. Without Homer, Hector would have been nothing. Without Klee, Walaschek wouldn't be anything. The good-for-nothings on the Servette team had already forgotten him, they didn't even wait for him to die first. But Klee . . . Because there's a moment when all the dead who have been forgotten, erased, and reduced first to a shadow of a shadow and then to nothing, to vapor dispelled by the first puff of wind, take notice, because their entire lives are at stake, for eternity.

So the dream was: would there be someone for me, will there? Please come! Oh Berkeley of the *esse est percipi*, deliver me from the limbo of oblivion. From the gray weight that keeps me down in this pit.

In the dream, Eugene Walaschek prayed to Berkeley, to Mnemosyne, to Zeus, to all of Olympus, and the father of the gods agreed, nodding his sacred crown. Whence Fate slipped into the folds of a degenerate painter's mind the idea of taking a random page from the newspaper and randomly, fatefully painting letters of the alphabet on it, thereby crossing out, at random, fatefully, words, names. One name was to disappear by half. Walaschek.

Would that do? No, said Olympus. Just as people have to be told, Here in Pisa, here in the baptistry, we don't have just the "famous echo" enshrined in all the tourist guidebooks so that choruses of tourists in shorts and suspenders can let out choruses of boisterous Os: we also have—look up, you sons of idiots—some Giovanni Pisano, see? his arch-stones full of archimandrites? just as in Lugano the herds of tourists have to be told, Here's Selmoni's column; just as in Bern, given the limitations of the small-brained, someone will have to tell all the space-cases, the masses of burger-flippers' kids who compulsively don't go to museums: Look—in a corner of that painting over there in the corner, which will soon be taken down and put in a storeroom, a man, a soccer player, is asking, as Electra did Zeus, not to die completely. Nothing more, nothing less.

This is Genia Walaschek's entire dream, but it's a dream that will last forever, if the Bern-Geneva InterCity train takes forever to bring old Walaschek back home, back to Geneva from Bern, back to his wife, fifty years after the final game of the Swiss Cup at the Wankdorf Stadium in Bern.

Thus the Ministers of Fate up in the Tall Towers Above the Clouds sent an errand boy to go to the loculus marked W and grab the Walaschek file. After a brief discussion, they unanimously decided on a special gift. In a new Resolution, per the appeal of Mr. Walaschek (redacted), and per the previous Resolution (redacted), we decree . . .

They decreed that one of the god Atramentous' scribes, whose name begins with the letter that had beheaded Walaschek—or rather, cut Walaschek in half from the middle up, saving the schek and destroying the Wala—that is, with O, would assist the painter in his work of salvation.

The O, fifteenth in the alphabet, isn't the most fruitful letter. But then, it could have been Ovid who was selected to give Walaschek eternal life:

> *Walaschek si Maeonium uatem sortita fuisses,*
> *Penelopes esset fama secunda tuae:*
> *quantumcumque tamen praeconia nostra ualebunt,*
> *carminibus uiues tempus in omne meis.*

> If you, Walaschek, had been assigned to Homer,
> Penelope's fame would be second to yours:
> Yet in so far as my praise has any power,
> you will still live, for all time, in my verse.

And it could have been, easily, with just a slightly harder push—as in the raffles at village festivals, when the wheel turns and the eyes of the villagers and villageresses are collectively glued to the board to see what number comes up. If it'd come up 16, the man tells the woman, I'd-a-won, by one number . . . If it'd come up 16, it could have been Petrarch, Pushkin, Pindar—the great Pindar, who any soccer player would have wanted:

> For if a man takes delight in toil and expenditure,
> and so succeeds in god-framed exploits,
> and if a divine power plants in him the pleasure of fame,

he drops his anchor at the furthest limits of happiness,
honored by the gods. With feelings such as these
 the son of Jenny Morel
prays to encounter Hades and to accept gray old age;
I appeal to Clotho on her high throne, and her sister
 Fates,
to agree with the noble commands of my friend.

Why is it that only the bloody and bloodthirsty—who have
crude and cruel blood in them right down to their feces—enter into the annals of posterity? "Unser Führer ist ein grosser
Künstler," a great artist, they, Hitler's guides in the Uffizi, said
to make sure they were overheard, a few days after the Wankdorf game between the Grasshoppers and Servette. But the ex-
painter and his cronies had kept Manet, Cézanne, Van Gogh,
et al, out of the museums . . . sold, evicted those deleterious
examples, degenerates like Klee and the primitivists. And from
June 1 of 1933 on, even the *Corriere della sera*, in German, an-
nounced "in jedes deutsches Heim gehört eine Büste unseres
Führers Adolph Hitler. Naturgetreues Kunstwerk . . . Volktüm-
licher Preis, Lit. 50." A bust in every house. A beyond-perfect
likeness. A steal. In vain did Hegel warn that there are portraits
whose likenesses are almost nauseatingly exact. People look at a
picture of a donkey on a postcard and say with satisfaction that
it resembles reality perfectly: yes, it's really a donkey. And the
cuckoo in the living room clock sounds just like a cuckoo. So
it's quite right for Hitler to be admired for eternity—as for the
others, too bad.

In less than two seconds, the computer of the gods—much more advanced than anything at NASA—went through more than 25,000 writers whose names begin with the letter O, Klee's fateful letter. As opposed to the sorts of things computers do down here, the computer of the gods, or of *Wille*, can compute attention, pain, hope, understanding, intention, sublime visions, ecstatic transport; and looking at the screen, up there, is like looking at an endless flock of doves taking flight over a bay.

The computer selected O/17360. It reported that this O was Klee's O, that 1736 was Klee's number in the cremation register at the Lugano crematory, with the addition of a zero derived from that selfsame mark of Klee's over Walaschek's name. Next to the O/17360 on the computer, a name appeared: "orelligiovanni." If only one less number had come up! Or even a few less. No need to go all the way back to Ovid: just to the poet Giorgio Orelli, for instance, he of the astute musical ear and the light touch in composing the sound of his sighs (Klee, if he had lived a little longer, would have been impressed); or else, one digit more, even without expecting to get to Ovid, there's Johann Caspar Orelli, the great philologist, who introduced to the Germans, among other things, the poets Campanella and Foscolo. A few digits further and we have the American sexophage O'Relly, or the nearly asexual and chaste Susanna Orelli, born in 1845 (and who died in 1939, so she would have been around long enough to read Walaschek's name not only in the April 19 *National Zeitung* but in all the papers, and perhaps also to have seen the name Paul Klee), who had married a Johann (= Giovanni) Orelli in 1879, already a bit old, a mathematician, soon deceased; beautiful and widowed too soon, she moved up in this society of eager drinkers (the Swiss); and when the country finally recognized her mission, legions of citizens and citizenesses too would soon pass their tongues, moistened and quick, over Susanna's back (or verso), the never-forgetful Post Office having effigied her, in profile, on a stamp: long live Susanna. Or, crossing the ocean and into painting, just a few digits less and it could have been one Gaston Orellana, who has observed the horror in the world so as not to contribute to it.

Nope. It came out orelligiovanni, O/17360.

No, Walaschek, having been born in Moscow in 1916, wasn't born under a lucky star. He opened his left eye just halfway. Then he drifted back to sleep.

He didn't dream of one of the American Edward O'Relly's (Orelli) sexercises isometric or isotonic but of a Swiss corporal three-fourths through the obstacle course, at those rocks that can pierce the groin just as the Christians were run though after being thrown off cliffs during the days of the legion of Martigny. The corporal grappled with a new recruit (scribe O/17360?) like a rove beetle with an earthworm. He chose the time and the place to fix him with the claws of his Ks:

– *E lü, ki ka l'è lü? Ke 'l s'anünciga!*

– And you, who are you! Identify yourself!

Yes, Walaschek may have been disappointed that *Wille* had chosen him—that rookie—as scribe. On the other hand, didn't Walaschek perhaps expect too much? That Apollo, that one of the nine muses, who? Calliope? would come down from Parnassus and Helicon just for him, bearing literary Nansen passports, and thus enter the brain of that scribe (one could have also called him, in the Swiss language—because the Swiss do what the pope does when he wishes Happy Easter *urbi et orbi* (on a smaller, on a miniature scale, that is)—saying Happy Easter in English, in Portuguese, in Korean, in Polish, in Russian too, in over thirty languages—whereas we, in the three official languages of Switzerland, could have called him a *löli*, a *chaibe löli*, a *tschumpel*, a *schnöderi*, a *morveux*, a *narigiatt*, a *gnolon*, a *mangiamuco*: which is to say, a nincompoop . . .); and once inside (the brain of O/17360) perhaps suggest how he should sing Walaschek, the *Schwarze pastose Wasserfarbe auf bedrucktem Zeitungspapier*, Klee's dancing alphabet? Like the prompter from his corner feeds the libretto's words to the tenor? Or else that river and wood nymphs would come to sit on his (the scribe's) knees, to stroke his brow something like Thetis did with Zeus's chin—he was delighted with her solicitations, just a tad worried about Hera: don't let her see you, oh! that busybody—bringing him into their circle of Oreads and Nereids and doing a nice rondeau for him?

Sure, the rondeau of the rotten egg.

O may thousands upon thousands of poets, from A to Z, in the guise of plumed angels with wax wings, astride gingerbread horses or mules, ride over to him and recite with him a hymn, an ode, a poem, to the football with the dynamic violence and grace impressed therein by Walaschek, the torsion of all the muscles in his body—just like when an act of God floods the universe and washes over all creatures, immerses them: wherever they are, there it is; it precedes them, accompanies them, follows them. One has only to yield to its waves. The ball will fly past the defensive line in mockery, it will elude the goalkeeper's catlike leap and hit the ropes of the net, where the poles meet.

No. The Olympus computer, *Wille*, didn't exactly favor Walaschek one hundred percent.

Mortal aims befit mortal men,

as Pindar once cautioned, and so farewell, country, Walaschek seemed to say, looking up at the sky with eyes full of disappointment, as when the ball flies past the defense perfectly but lands three centimeters too high or hits a pole, the goalie stranded, and the crowd's O, long and hoarse . . .

With all the ifs of the insatiable. If only it had been Horace (*Orazio!*), says a Latinist, Antonius Stilus, slapping his thigh like Dante's farmer. Horace was also a farmer's son, but a noble farmer from Rome; he's astute, obstinate, honest yet quite sly, coarse, and wise, with keen senses and vulgar impulses—a born joker, his thumbs firm in his pockets and his soul firm in its place, vital; he could keep his slave-girl in a hall of mirrors and then study, in slow motion, on instant replay, that refined forward of eros and poiesis. The ifs, the regrets, the mimetic reconstructions (instant replay) of the strike, the dart, the jaculum (in the ejaculation), failed: at night, in the cafés all the way to the osterias on the port. If, if, if . . .

If it had been Pindar—ah, Pindar!

But the ancient
splendor sleeps; and mortals forget

what does not attain poetic wisdom's choice pinnacle,
yoked to glorious streams of verses.
Therefore celebrate in a sweetly sung hymn
Strepsiades too, and Eu Genia Walaschek.

With a central triad like Walaschek, Belli, and Trello, these lambdas dancing their lambada switch back and forth in a bewildering whirlwind, *concordia discors* all the way to the opponent's net (for Walaschek could have worn number 10 as well as number 8), Pindar could have dashed off another triumphal Isthmian. Belli, the center forward, was French and, as such, was able to spend several months as a guest at the Stalag IV-F in Germany, with prisoner number 36293. He became Swiss only later. Trello (hypocorism for André) Abegglen was Xam's (palindrome of Max) brother, who was center forward for the Grasshoppers, the opposing team. Trello begged his Servette teammates, before the second final, not to do anything to his brother. Is this mercy the reason for their defeat?

Pindar could have sung this drama of Trello's: fraternal love in conflict with national interest.

No, Klee's O would not be picked up by Pindar like the gold ring of a bride who dances all whitedressed on her wedding day. It was dented, detached from its chain, and nobody could foresee where it would wind up; like those guys who pound beers on their way to the stadium, far away from their familial chains; and a pleasant warmth rises first to their heads, then drops down to their groins, and they want to roll around on the ground, yell, rip the white gowns off every bride. And since the other team made a goal within the first ten minutes they wanted to take an iron bar in their hands and whack the heads off every swan in the lake.

One of them, in the top section of the stands, stood up and ripped off his checkered shirt, baring his chest and looking around with fierce, ferocious eyes. Everyone was yelling out insults and shoving each other. If it didn't come to a tie there would be a mess. The people in the fortieth row might jump onto the ones in the thirty-ninth and start a huge brawl, fists flying like the letters of a mad alphabet, as in the painting by Paul Klee.

Io tengo una pistola caricata, the bride's friends sang, the last ones at the reception, all a little drunk with their white shirts wrinkled.

Io tengo sei fratelli, con gli occhi bianchi e neri, io tengo sei fratelli, t'ammazzeranno.

They'll kill you. Isn't it easy to kill, perhaps? For some people it's a banality, harder to say than to do, dixit Caesar (to Metellus), in Rome after the Rubicon. At the mere thought, however, Professor Syntax, a boor at home, albeit a highly esteemed colleague at the Academy of Schoolteachers, removed his hat and mopped his vast brow. You can grow up and spend two thirds of your life with the belief, almost the certainty, that you'd never hurt a fly (well, admittedly, at least a European fly; the problem arises, if at all, with African, Asian ones, idem for spiders, etc.), then one day go and find yourself, just by pure chance, in the lobby of a building on a somewhat seedy street. To enter or not to enter, that is the question. Whether 'tis . . . After all, the schoolteacher could do it for scientific reasons. The word "scientific" is, in the twentieth century, and not only in the brain of Professor Syntax, the ultimate pass against every "halt, who goes there?" A teacher knows that to possess is one thing, to be possessed another. *Homo sum, nihil humani a me alienum puto.* I am a man; nothing human is foreign to me. Even if the schoolteacher didn't go around, as he should have, with an iron-tipped cane. He was about to enter when he felt a hand, like a waft of spring wind, brush his head. He turned, curious, and saw a tall blond young man with a dirty smiling face waving his hat up high and spitting at the schoolteacher derisively. He was holding Professor Syntax's hat like a Yashin with the ball he could block with the utmost ease, holding it well above the reach of his adversaries' heads, ready to throw it with both hands to the first of his to break free. Indeed, the blond adolescent threw the hat to another companion who passed it, at chest-level, to a third, that one to a fourth, and so on, with their dizzying Brazilian-style stalling maneuvers, and so the hat went back to the blond man with the dirty face, the one who had first snatched it from Professor Syntax in that red-light lobby, who started the others throwing it just centimeters away from the schoolteacher's completely flushed face. It was flushed with shame and rage; he could have had a heart attack. This had to be Zamora, a student, a descendant of the famous Spanish goalkeeper, who with his left hand would seize the ball in the fray near the goal and with his right (or vice versa) would shove with cunning or even jab his fist into the throat or the scowling mug of the bulldog center forward, who deserved nothing less; who steps in front of you, that *hijo de puta*, with his leg out, or his knee poised to knee you in the jewels, in the lower abdomen, in the—sorry, excuse my language, but it must be said—in the balls. Professor Syntax heard—he felt like he heard—the old resident Methuselah who, very very softly, almost as if issuing a threnody from the hereafter on low batteries, saying to the hooligans: Leave the poor man in peace, can't you see that he could be your grandfather?

   – Call . . . the schoolteacher cried out. He realized he hadn't finished his sentence, that is, that he was no longer a teacher here.

   – Huh? huh? said the Resident Methuselah, apparently stone deaf. Luckily, the teacher hadn't completely lost his head, so he was able to come to his senses: "Yeah," he told himself, "great idea, call the police, that way you'll end up in the local papers and look like a pig for the rest of your days, and then, post mortem, they'll remember you as a pig."

   So he sank onto some sort of bench in that lobby, it too having ended up there, that nasty thing, by the will of Schopenhauer's *Wille*, and in seeing that milksop knocked down, one of the hooligans with a Judah's face, interrupting their Brazilian game, planted himself in front of the teacher, opened the zipper of his faded jeans, soiled his hat, then took that hat all dirty and damp with dank and rank humors and flung it into the highest, furthest corner of that lobby. As to a felled Don Quixote, so to the schoolteacher, poetry, refuge of the defeated, came to mind:

> With humors dank and rank
> gush indiscreet springs.

It was a brief moment of weakness, of *catastroika*. As he saw that the hooligans were leaving the "field," the schoolteacher felt something welling up deep inside him, something that had never welled up before. He dragged himself to the edge of the lobby where there was a wide staircase directly overlooking the sidewalk. He saw that the hooligans were going down, skipping athletically, tired of the hat and its owner, already on to other enterprises, other targets.

– Hey you, the teacher shouted, hey you . . .

No one turned. So the teacher stuck his left hand in his pocket, and having found a few coins he closed them in his fist and hurled them vehemently at the boys, already in the street, without hitting them.

But if it had been a revolver he'd have pulled the trigger. He said to himself: "Yes!" And so he didn't so much sit as plunk down onto the top stair of that staircase. What worried the other Methuselah a little about that atrium, the one who tore the entrance tickets and who, in order to avoid trouble, came over and, seeing the teacher prostrate but unharmed, said like a tried and true member of the golden-years set: – Dumb kids today. Vulgar. Nothing to do and nowhere to go. What are we coming to? You know what I say? Pay no attention, go inside and watch your movie, fill your head with something else. See your little minxes.

He didn't even let him launch into the catalogue of delights. With an agility at which he was the first (and only) to be surprised, he found himself back on the street. He didn't worry about recovering his soiled hat; he would brandish his bare head on that dicey side street. What should he do? Buy a beheading bowler like Oddjob's in *Goldfinger*? An actual gun? If it were Sunday and not Friday, he would have gone to the stadium. No. Lassie, come home. Back to the fields, Bigio. Everyone, at least once a year, should make a pilgrimage, not to Santiago de Compostela or Lourdes, but to one of the great temples of football, where the violent hooligans transform into a riotous mass, the same who had paid him honor that Friday, at three o'clock P.M. The Ninth Hour. He closed his eyes.

On the stands they also lit smoky fires and shot firecrackers and hurled coins onto the playing field. Their curses were those of soldiers on the attack, the difference being that soldiers shoot, they have to. Tatatatatatata . . . at a much faster rhythm than a Lempen racing toward the opposing team's goal, carrying the globe on his forehead, balanced between a Siberian nose and a forehead probably deformed by the forceps like a mound by a bulldozer.

In Switzerland the stadiums are never overflowing with oceanic crowds. Switzerland is often insulted and vilified for—they say—preaching morality from their high horse, for living in peace and pantofles—they say—without any more William Tells or the heroes of Novara and Marignano. And yet old Homer would praise Switzerland for not wanting to break the peace, unlike the power-hungry Greek aristocrats. Old Homer would praise Sindelar and recommend him for the Nobel Peace Prize. In memoriam! He tried as hard as he could to lead the people in the stadiums of the world to a vision of harmony and beauty and not to bestiality.

– Bestiality? the butcher, Enrico il Piccolo, jumped in. Bestiality, you say? But beasts don't point a gun at your head, they don't pull the trigger as if they were just swatting a fly. Beasts are better than us. Beasts only resemble us in hunger or sex. Take a billy goat. Male like all males. He's the only male in a herd of nanny goats. But if he meets another herd of a hundred nanny goats with its single billy goat, the two goats begin to duel. To the death. Which isn't to say rough, but to say that they can keep going until one of their cranial vaults splits. All this in silence, because goats, unlike men, not being made in God's image and likeness, do not have the gift of language. Not even to swear. The only sounds are the dull, fast, and quickly executed blows of butting horns. Their eyes are similar to those of human males, but they look like fake glass in fake rings.

And when one of the two goats falls, it's like when it snows, soft, in the mountains; it seems like God is taking the opportunity to make a round of inspections throughout the world, and God's visit strikes a bit of fear into the hearts of men.

It wasn't snowing in the stadium and the enraged fans ripped out bars, handrails—they would have grabbed the I-beams if they could. Paramedics stood discreetly on the sidelines. The nervousness of the mothers idem.

In Vienna, a little cloud drifted through the Viennese sky. The Danube moved sluggishly toward the sea—the Black. A nurse in Vienna diligently went through a stack of files. Sindelar? Who was that? A proletarian poet, who died in 1938, not thinking of Sindelar, but as if he were, as he walked through a field, wondered, "But is it really possible not to doff your hat in the face of such beauty?" An invalid with amputated legs was looking at photos of actresses; he felt like whistling the "Lili Marlene": *unter der Laterne* . . . but a placard imposed silence. Another invalid was looking at old photos of star footballers. A third was crying and wasn't looking at anything.

Whereas at the stadium they were shouting and people were reaching automatically for their cigarettes. And when the time came for the penalty kick it was like a revolver being lifted to somebody's temple: is there a bullet or isn't there? But a few hours after the game, even in Paris in 1938, they could get gypsy violins. Could the Swiss, and Walaschek, having beaten Germany 4 to 2, grant themselves the luxury of a nightclub, of beer or champagne? No, gypsy violins it is. A soccer player has responsibilities to his country, and the Federal Council had sent a telegram of congratulations. Good job, boys. And as everyone was coming back from the stadium in the Parisian twilight, they asked one another, with incredulous glances, how these Swiss guys had managed to beat Hitler's Grossdeutschland. It was as if there were a beautiful sports pennant on the top of the Eiffel Tower on that evening of Parisian sport. Only the bus drivers and all the Parisian workers in general still wore their usual workaday expressions, with their eyes that seemed to say: we're neither German nor Swiss, we're just regular Frenchmen, regular Turks, regular Algerians. Like me, you got your ration of kicks in the ass today, but most of them were given politely, admit it! Anyway, it's better that Switzerland won.

Those who had played showed teammates and coaches the marks left by kicks to their shins. They recalled the elbows, the insults, the spit, the booing from the stands, warnings and penalties from the referee, defamatory insults bandied back and forth. But when you win all is forgotten. It's when you lose that you count every mote in your eye, like all the bitter pills you have to swallow in order to secure a post in the city administration, or some little insurance agency, or a newsstand or bar. The athletes' bar. It's not the place to attack the outside forward or take him down if he passes you. The customers aren't to be touched, you can't kick at

the customers' legs. Even on a rainy day, the ex-player, now manager of the bar, thinks: wipe your feet, you slob. His instinct was
to yell like Zenga or any other hothead goalie, giving instructions
as to where the defensive wall should be: to the right, more to the
right. The umbrella goes in the umbrella stand, what, have you got
slices of salami for eyes? Ah, if only he had a nice whistle like a
referee and could blow it from noon till night, pull out the yellow
card, then the red. But instead . . .

Instead: – Hello, Counselor! And smile at everybody. Greet everyone who enters and give them a hearty good-bye when they
leave. Exchange at least a word or two. See you later, good seeing
you. Talk about the weather? Go with the weather, even if it happens to be 1940. Talk about the championships? Sure, even if in
1940 the championships are mobilization competitions. His pre-
diction for Sunday? Sunday's a sure bet, we can't lose.

The ex-player, now manager and practically boss of the bar
(this isn't Walaschek, Walaschek would go into the finance administration of the city of Geneva) internalizes (as they say) what
people expect of him. O holy purge. It is you who prepares the
place for the god of athletes. O purity. O universal acceptance.
O unreserved submission! It is you who draws the god of sports
to the bottom of our hearts. And may their abilities be what they
desire, you are, lord of sport, my every good; make of this humble
being what you will, may he act, be inspired, be subject to your
impulses, all is one in all, and your all belongs to you, it comes
from you and acts in your stead. I no longer have anything to do
with it, not a single moment of my life depends on me, it all belongs to you, I have neither to add nor subtract anything, nor seek,

nor reflect. My task is to be satisfied with you, to take no action in anything, whether active or passive, but to leave everything to your will.

In truth, the ex-halfback turned bartender wanted to take action against an out-of-work fatso with a sallow Jewish face who always occupied a corner table for two hours sipping a tea down to its last drop. He would have happily locked him in the garage, enthusiastically shoved an air pump in his rear end and blown him up until he was as round as a balloon, then at nighttime loaded him in a truck and dumped him off a slope, listening to him roll all the way down dragging empty cans behind him. But he quickly chased those thoughts away. He returned to someone or another to talk about the team's new acquisitions.

– A Brazilian in his thirties.

– But doesn't that make him an old horse?

– We can do what Hitler did. Take over Holland and incorporate the tulips into the national team. All they have to do is go from orange to the white-crossed red. But this chitchat was of no interest to the scribe preselected by *Wille*, number O/17360, who, aware of being incapable of coming anywhere close to one of Pindar's Isthmians even with the shadow of his little toe, decided to do what he had been chosen for with diligence: if, with his *Alphabet I*, Klee wanted to express *a moment* of his interiority without conceding his privacy, his oracular voice—not using the tools (which he didn't have anyway) of a Kabbalistic exegete, of archetypes, of the numbers of the Apocalypse, he, Scribe O/17360, like any good wordsmith at a public gathering, recorded every interpretation, however crude—*cusa l'è che 'l vör dì*? the doorman of building 137 wondered out loud, unhesitantly, and his wife, in a faded blue smock like the ones worn by railmen shunting on the ramp, translated supportively: What's that supposed to mean? The eyes trained on the scribe said: you explain it, if you can.

And so Scribe O/17360, like a good schoolteacher, glossed: Klee's dislocated letters on the page from the April 19, 1938 *National Zeitung* swim like fish in an aquarium, a big parallelepiped bowl in the lobby of a luxury hotel, and the fish are in their turn the image, the emblem, the symbol (do you understand what I mean, kids?) of the human condition—they could be men and women crossing a square: Red, de la Concorde, St. Peter's, Parade, of the blessed banks, of the ring: the Ring. It's futile, irrelevant to ask what was going through their minds as they crossed the squares, as they went through their circumscribed everyday motions (children, do you remember the complement of circumscribed motion? Which is not the same as the complement of direction and certainly not the complement of location?): Work? Love? Money? Staying out all night? Killing? Is Klee's O the grindstone of the knifegrinder with his own circumscribed motion, standing at the corner of the square, sharpening knives, all of them, for anyone who asks; is it the tambourine of an acrobat or a fire-eater? A monk's tonsure that, seen from one of the spires of the cathedral, looks like an O bobbing toward the cathedral door? The cathedral that's on one side of the rectangular square?

Or is it the O of horror, of fire? A cannon placed in the middle of the square, instead of the usual horse, the usual hero: a howitzer, ornament and splendor of our age; an otolaryngologist looks deep down into the cannon's throat and bursts out with the joy of someone who feels like rejoicing thus:

Ooooooooooooooh

– No, try to say *ah*—I can see better that way.

In his generosity, Klee showed great pity on the poor scribe. Amicably, he put his hand on his shoulder and walked with him under the plane tree on the square.

– My friend, don't wear yourself out. You don't have to explain my O. The greatest fortune that can befall an author is not to be read, a painter not to be seen, or to be seen with haste, like on those horrendous group museum tours: as long as the work is talked about, obviously. Or, if they see you, if they read you, you're fortunate to be misunderstood. If they understand you, no one will think you're right; if they don't understand you, everyone will project onto you their inchoate desires, their secret dreams. And your success is assured. You have to be mysterious, like a witch or an astrologer, people have always had a need for magicians and sorcerers. He paused briefly and said: *Diesseitig bin ich gar nicht fassbar.* No, I truly cannot be grasped. How can one make the masses understand the combination of the physis of the Greeks, the psyche of Christianity, and your tiny self? I too have a bit of the obscurity of my luminous contemporary— Einstein, I mean.

– So your O is everything and nothing?

Klee opened his arms. Clever and honest as he was, he said:

– Sometimes I envy Mondrian—the ascetic, the pure, the geometry of his straight lines. What does it mean? people say, bending over the placard while the sweat-soaked paterfamilias searches in the catalog purchased at the entrance. Mondrian uses titles like *Landscape, Reclining* (or standing) *Nude, Meditation I* or two or twenty-seven thousand, or *Himalaya*. As long as he doesn't put cretin pig illiterate imbecile idiot pinhead in ecstasy, since the viewer wants to know exactly what our friend Adolf wanted to know during his tour of the Uffizi in the spring of '38—he asks, like a police officer, like a guard, for the generalities—and if the painting says: "Our Adolf, Pinhead in Ecstasy," he would take offense. Someone from the bench against the back wall asked:

– And what about Walaschek, didn't he ever ask you anything?

Klee knit his brow. Scribe O/17360 replied, serious and sure:

– No, he ever asked me anything.

On the way back to Geneva from Bern (the party in honor of Karl Rappan, inventor of the "bolt" strategy and coach for the national team that beat Hitler's Germany in Paris in '38, a half century later, had been wonderful: they all posed instinctively, several times, in various positions, for photographers and TV cameras, six of them standing with folded arms and the other five squatting in front), Walaschek had closed his eyes to rest his head and to enjoy the grace with which the InterCity train raced from Bern through the domestic Fribourg plains, the vineyards over Laussane. He opened them every now and then "to see where we are," just as in life he liked to have a proper view of the game (also known as philosophy). On a little field outside Fribourg two teams of men were playing. White jerseys and yellow jerseys. The train, going along at full speed, had allowed him to see only little, but in that little he had immediately spotted a flaw: they were all chasing after the ball too much. They lacked a coach's hand, a midfielder's brain, a midfielder like Sirio Vernati, shining with bright light, or, modesty aside, an inside forward like him, Walaschek: an inside forward who was of the old school, à la Vonlanthen, *alla volante*, at the wheel, weaving patterns and spreading wings, freeing the divine Sindelar with a long pass: he, the forward, changes the game, seeming to run and run only because, in the air, he makes the ball fly.

In any case, tomorrow he'll buy the newspapers and in the evening he'll watch the TV—maybe it'll just be on for a minute, but one can't expect too much. They said all kinds of things. The German-speakers, during their toasts, spoke in Swiss-German and went on and on about why Swiss-German is spoken in German Switzerland and not Germany. The Swiss-Frenchman spoke about the hardships of the Swiss-French threatened by the Swiss-Germans. The most optimistic player present was the one who spoke the third national language, Italian. He said, citing a poet, that "the dark days are passed." Carducci!

– Carducci? Who was that?

Scribe O/17360 prompted, under his breath: He's the Lion of the Maremma, Bolognese by election, decorated—just think!—with the Nobel in literature. It would be like mentioning the name Colaussi (actually Colausig), Serantoni, those dazzling Petronians— i.e,. Bolognese—two-time world champions on Vittorio Pozzo's lucky team. Yet just try and ask a young person today who Colaussi/Colausig was. Ignoramuses, asses of the new Arcadia, who are in need of—if you'll allow me to again cite Carducci, and as you can see, by memory—threshing-thrashings in the morning, noon, afternoon, and night. The dark days are passed.

The one snickering this time was Marc Vuilleumier, who knew all about the negotiations with the German authorities regarding the letter J to be stamped on non-Aryans' passports. But Vuilleumier, who at one time could have testified on this matter for hours and hours, was intent on specifying that just because things were different, that didn't mean we could just sanctify ourselves with a few swings of the thurible. Scribe O/17360 was called to testify: he had the floor.

Scribe O/17360 just wanted to add that even long after the war, Erasmus and Montaigne—and not only those two—would have been appalled to see what was happening on the frontiers of the nations of Europe. That the shutters on every shop were closed from '39 to '45 could serve as additional proof for the residents of Lugano and environs of the felicitous choice of their most intelligent forefathers of 1798, *patria est ubicumque est bene*: a farmer from Ponte Tresa, Switzerland could look after his vineyard, and the farmer a few meters away, from Ponte Tresa, Italy, after going to Eritrea and Somalia, could end up in Albania, to be a Cyrenian in Cyrene, in Ukraine, could go to the devil, could wind up yawning out his soul in Buchenwald at the feet of rotten gods. But that's later. Let me tell you, the scribe said, about the cows of Pedrinate.

In the twentieth century, the cows of the civilized world, and not only those in Pedrinate—even though men continue to shrewdly exploit them—should have learned to consult an atlas. They should have learned to read a book on rhetoric, something by Lausberg, acquaint themselves a little with the meaning of symbols: what is a chain-link fence? It can be a physical thing or a metaphysical thing. And anyone who illegally crosses a chain-link fence, the "metal net" (it could also be barbed wire), is either a "metal-muncher," i.e., an immigrant fresh over the fence, or a smuggler, a deserter, a snitch, a spy, some kind of shirker, someone to subject to a hundredth-degree interrogation, imprisonment, someone to send off to a forced labor camp. But the cows of Pedrinate hadn't read a single text by Hoepli or Treccani or Lausberg, nothing. Thus on the night between the 29th and 30th of May 1983, nice and easy—or as Erasmus (who was horrified by borders) would say, *gradatim, paulatim, pedetentim*—they crossed the border. You should know, my dear fellows, that Pedrinate is a small village where Little Red Riding Hood's mother could have lived. Pedrinate is the name of the southernmost town in Switzerland. It lies on the border with Italy. It's right above Chiasso. And as a few local newspapers mention (here, we'll take the *Gazzetta Ticinese* from June 2, 1983), and as a letter from the City of Chiasso dated October 17, 1989 confirms, there was, that night, an "illegal entry" in Pedrinate.

So during the night between May 29th and 30th of 1983, in the full bloom of spring, "four young cows (heifers) and two young bulls crossed over from Italy." Those crazy kids! one might think, to avert the association of *vacche*—cows—with whores, prostitutes, when everybody knows or should know that real cows only couple with males once a year, purely for reproductive purposes, if they're not artificially inseminated! in homage to a horrid (to no one) zootechnical racism (and if nonetheless this point bothers anyone, remember *ad abundantiam* that in the kingdom of heaven we'll be preceded by publicans and prostitutes anyway). But to abolish on the spot all syllogism, or rather, enthymeme, the news column reports the cause: "Four cows (mooo moooo) and two bulls, *residents* of Parè (Italy), were found on the fields of Pedrinate (Switzerland) grazing *with relish* on the first fruits of the vines and various crops" (the italics are Scribe O/17360's, to emphasize the fact that "residents" is typically used to denominate the border-dwellers who cross over for work, and who are supported and coveted by the economy; that the sinful and illicit lust in the world is incommensurable—it affects animals too); and it carries, most importantly, certain consequences: "A walk in the countryside that cost the owner a thousand francs for the customs fine alone" (this the newspaper's version). The newspaper concludes: "One is most astonished by the complete absence of border patrols in the area," whereas the official version—that is, the only completely reliable one—from the City of Chiasso, Switzerland, says that the owner "paid a fee of 1200 francs to cover the damages reported by the owners of crops and vineyards, customs fees, and transport costs." All things considered, for a local, paying 1200 francs in fines is as easy as going from Pescarenico (Como) to Rimini on foot: and that's quite a walk! With that, the six daredevils (if you'll allow a half-juvenile, half-animal metaphor, at any rate antipodean to reasonable adults) "sheltered in the stables of the city butcher's in Chiasso (. . .) with the assistance of one of the offended parties" could be loaded onto a trailer. Thus the owner "had them cross the border via the same route they'd come by."

Nothing is said in the news summary or the official report about the breed of the six bovine masterminds, nor whether among the fruit grazed upon "with relish" there were forbidden herbs. Were they the brown Schwyz (from the very heart of Switzerland), or black (like the Haute-Valaisians) or spotted—whether white and red as in Emmental, or black and white as in Gruyère, or scrawny-dirty-white as in the Maremma? Undoubtedly the farmer from Parè was cut from the same cloth as the farmer from Pedrinate. But the names of the animals from Parè were perhaps more imaginative than those from Pedrinate, because a farmer loves to give his animals—when they must be "christened," that is—names that might evoke essential moments in his own life. The life of a farmer from Parè has different coordinates from those of a farmer from Pedrinate. Thus it is not impossible to venture that with the six names of the six metal-munching animals one could have made not an entire team but half a team, as if split by Paul Klee's paintbrush, of what they call a defensive line:

Mersa   Matrouh
Guadalquivir   Croatia
Tripoli   Al-Jaghbub   Tobruk
. . . .

Now almost everyone was laughing a little, except for Asshat with his military wedge cap, and everyone seemed to be imploring Scribe O/17360 not to spread too much (negative) publicity about the cows from Pedrinate, otherwise that sort of clandestine border crossing could catch on—birds, snakes, flies, badgers, hares, worms, all pretending to be ignorant of the particularities of customs regulations.

– Noooo! That can't be true!

There goes old Can't-Be-True, Giuseppe, Sepp, a.k.a. Can't-Be-True, because he'd spent his entire life in astonishment at everything, and his ninetieth birthday was just around the corner. Someone would mention something that was going on in the world, something out of the paper, and he'd put his hand behind his right ear (he didn't trust the left) and yell through his thick white beard: – Noooo! That can't be true.

– Listen to this one, the first thumbsucker said, listen to this, Giuseppe:

There's a peasant woman who needs to give birth and, to help her body along, she goes up the mountain and comes back down with a load of ninety kilos, and that same night, ninety divided by thirty, she brings into the world, in half an hour, three big babies, all boys, one after the other, in a row, one, two, three . . .

– No, it can't be!

– How 'bout this one? You know how long it took Hitler to take over Austria?

– How long, tell me!

– Fifteen minutes!

– No, I don't believe it.

– What do you mean you don't believe it. Look at this. He pointed to the newspaper.

– Impossible.

They told him that in the next World Cup there was going to be a Mediterranean team made up of all women.

– No, impossible.

– What's that supposed to mean, impossible? You think I'd tell you something that wasn't true? The stopper, the center back, will be Phryne.

– Phryne?

– What world do you live in, Giuseppe? Don't you read the newspaper? They were about to convict her in court, and her lawyer, seeing the wanton woman hopeless, tore her misfortunes clean off her body. She was left completely naked and nobody wanted to convict her. Free, a clam at sea.

– Nooo, that doesn't even sound a little true.

He ran his tongue over his dry lips, his moustache.

– They're going to have cyclamen-violet jerseys and the flag of Cyprus. It's the Venus team, listen up:

Lilith

Nefertiti   Judith

Ipsitilla   Phryne   Iphigenia

Myrrha   Lesbia   Tamar   Phaedra   Yael

A few of them looked perplexed. A Judith, a Yael, would be capable of sending you to whichever Holofernes happens to be on hand strutting around by the corner flag, of sending you to Beelzebub's infirmary after five minutes of play. Either way, it's pitch invasion.

– I'd like to see that, said Can't-Be-True. I won't miss it on TV. What'd you say the name was of that one who plays buck naked?

They were all cracking up, save Klee, because Klee had been dead for a while: since 1940. He died on the 29th of the month of June, at 7:30 A.M., "due to heart disease (myocarditis). Burial may be permitted, 24 hours having passed since death. Staff Physician Dr. H. Bodmer."

Klee would no longer draw the interminable, the radiant, that which is irreducible to a prime number; vertiginous, a cavity-unfathomability-hiding place for the innocent, before or after the devastations of life, to play hide-and-seek in; that softest, most delicate, heavenly spiral: Phryne's navel. Epicenter of the world. Give me a place to stand, Phryne's navel, and I can move the world!

He would no longer be able to draw an entire family of worms on the way to Mass in single file with all their little Catholic wormlings, or like so many little Jews, ornate kippahs on their little heads. Like an ensemble of acrobats, clowns, like marines or little kittens sliding under the chain-link fence in Pedrinate that neatly separates Switzerland and Italy, in single file, one by one, they invade the holy land of the Ticino. Not the wild rabbits, hares, nor foxes, nor the badger that, like a smuggler, passes through the holes made by the smugglers, nor an "enterprising animal" (*Unternehmendes Tier*, 1940) breaking through the breach that's like the Dutch sea after the Dutch blew up the dams at the Nazis' approach.

Klee was dead. He had not seen the early nor the late sun on that July 29th, nor the camellias oblivious to the war, nor the violet of the wisteria creeping up the walls in the country and up toward the hills in Brione all the way down to Mergoscia—where the people still lived a life which, in the account of His Majesty's acolyte Sir Thomas Hobbes, was: nasty, brutish, and short; people who, before dinner on spring-summer evenings, sat on their stone steps in droves, like bees out for air, their stingers at rest—or at windows climbing over thin walls up to a balcony with laundry out to dry, up to a roof on top of which, perhaps, waves one of the innocent flags Klee was so fond of; that lavish violet wisteria of Locarno, Muralto, Burbaglio, where a fisherman's daughter lived, *la pessàta*, the fish-seller. Oh, if only Klee could have gone back to Burbaglio ten years later, in 1950, to see *la pessàta* in all her sixteen years, and so could have reproduced an April in Burbaglio, Spring in the center with a poignant gait making her way toward the Piazza Grande, and everyone turning to look at her—and she knew it, walking like a queen who has the whole city at her feet. Klee would no longer be able to put in his painting in emulation of Sandro Botticelli contra Botticelli the girl from Burbaglio with her Olympic step, smooth hair, firm breasts, her sex still like a wren or a robin hopping and disappearing into the branches on the shore of the lake, still a shore to all, by waters still limpid for all. With her own mortal name. She was the striking Carmen Mariotta, and surrounding her were the three graces, Miss Ilaria Crivelli, Miss Silvana Gianola, and Miss Elena Reggiori, and even when they were sitting in a boat they were tall and svelte; but Klee, in the last spring of his life, his last stay in the Burbaglio light, was only able to draw the supine, submerged, as if dead, *Kranker im Boot*, a 1940 sick man in the boat of 1940.

Miss Carmen Mariotta (a little girl in June 1940) grew up to be the reincarnation, physically speaking, of Phryne. And on her way home from the Piazza Grande everyone turned to look at her, and she knew it! Like the wisteria, she had the grace and airy yet controlled whimsy, the full sound, low to the ground, of the cello in the *moderato* of the concerto for cello and orchestra in C major, Hob. VIIb: 1, Haydn.

Klee would never see another bee, a flower, the fish-seller with her beautiful smooth hair. Never again would he play his beloved violin.

He was cured of life. He would never again draw soldiers brusquely awakened at daybreak in that late 1940 June in the barracks, and then led to a pass, with the nausea that comes with the wee hours of the morning, still cold, with a chance of rain or sleet in the mountains, the last burst of spring before it turns to summer. The soldiers sat, jostling, against the back of the truck, as if cataphracted in their oversized gray coats, holding their rifles between their knees, up to their helmets; and in the mouth of the barrel—a nice O—they've each put a flock of cotton, like a white flower, so that rain won't get inside and rust the barrel.

On one of those evenings when the damned spring was sliding into summer, there was one among those soldiers who, they say, had just completed basic training; and on the evening of the dinner for the entire company, as is customarily arranged by command to celebrate those young men's promotion to the rank of soldier (analogous to confirmation, which promotes the soldiers of Christ), he had accumulated pains that were difficult to endure— not physical pains, but a wave that swelled in his brain, on the verge of overflowing just like a stream in a downpour—bad news from home, his girlfriend with someone else, a future that demoralized him no matter which way he looked at it, examining it like a mason does a misshapen stone; and so during dinner and after he intentionally, immoderately, beyond his limits, drank. So when they brought him back to quarters, amid the smell of old straw, debris from the lanterns, all the noise in the dormitory that, between the drunk and otherwise, couldn't be too big, as he slipped under his filthy covers he felt a cadenced, progressive crescendo of chaos in his head. In flashes of mad lucidity he felt that his being was coming apart: it wasn't physical pain, not even in his legs, which were stiff from too much alcohol—it was the pain of being a part of being, immense—a cosmic, catholic, ecumenical hemorrhage. But his den-mate, a Lepontian called Quinto, a skilled handler of the crooked things in life, a great drinker who could always maintain self-control (in part because of his great physical strength), realized what was going on, and with his authority and muscle and expertise gave quick instructions to the two neighbors on either side as to how to assist this needy man who looked like a calf at death's door, and since he knew that noise in such moments is a lethal additive to alcohol, a poison that goes straight through the middle of the brain and quarters it, he imposed absolute silence on everyone, on each and every one, as if there, at that moment, the culmination of the party, an atom bomb had exploded.

But Klee would no longer be able to draw the miraculous silence of that company of men because Klee was dead. Nor the O of a stadium with so many little Os inside from the open mouths suddenly mute as if at someone's command to silence them all at once and out of the blue, seized with horror in the face of collective intoxication, the pain having reached a measure beyond measure, and with the even smaller Os of the eyes, cavernous Os in those circles of faces, eighty thousand faces in the stadium stands, in the ring around the field—all of them dumbstruck by what was happening down there, on mother earth in that early July 1940. Because Paul Klee was dead.

On the field, just down below, was a formation like this:

In the middle, at attention, the team of referees: Fate, *Wille*, and Providence. On the opposite side, the mouths of cannons at the ready:

He would no longer paint the black sky on a blue summer's night; his painting becomes air, sky, even when he uses black: not one but twenty-seven blacks, I assure you—like Van Gogh said. Now perhaps Klee's up, up on a little cloud, talking about black and Rembrandt to Van Gogh. Talking about playing with color, making an argument with a line, expressing an idea with a title.

Paul Klee hadn't been fortunate—if we consider such a thing significant—in the selection of his date of death. Because on June 29th, a Saturday, the feast day of Saints Peter and Paul, the newspapers in ultra-Catholic Italian Switzerland don't come out. Therefore, we don't even know what time the sun rose (his last!), though we can infer that it was around 4:32, because on the 28th,

St. Irenaeus's day, it rose at 4:31 and on July 1st, the day of his cremation, at 4:33. When the newspapers were issued again, on Monday July 1st, they had lots of other things to talk about.

Hitler went to Paris, Mussolini visited the Western Front, the Maddalena Pass, the Col de Tende, inspected the grunts and blackshirts (the twenty-eighth type of black, never contemplated by Van Gogh) who took part in the hundred-hours' battle—not much more, though still more than Germany's fifteen minutes for Austria—June 21st, 22nd, 23rd, 24th, and a bit of the 25th. The order to cease fire came at thirty-five minutes past midnight; in Germany celebrations broke out, while the entire city of Tripoli was mourning the death of Italo Balbo; like Rome, at Caligula's death, *vasta silentio*; like Tarascon at the death (which turned out to be a false alarm) of Tartarin. Having died a day before Klee, at the same clinic in Muralto, Sant'Agnese, Mr. Max Emden, owner of the Brissago Islands—he'd get at least a mention in the news. But unlike Klee, he had *bought* Ticinese citizenship as well as local residency in Ronco sopra Ascona. Even Karl Knie, business director of the Circus Knie, had made it into the news, having been gravely wounded when the hunting rifle he was cleaning accidentally went off. But no such luck for Klee. If he had lived a few days longer, he would have been able to feverishly draw the Maginot Line visited by Hitler during those days, or the sirens that went off right on the day of his death, June 29th, even if not for him—in fact, there was an announcement in the Friday the 28th paper: "Tomorrow, the last Sunday of the month, the emergency siren test will be conducted"—or the reunion of the generation of 1878 (even that didn't work out for him, having been born in '79) for, as the newspaper said, "Everyone born in 1878 in Lugano and environs is invited to attend a meeting at Bar Golf, to discuss their 62nd birthday celebration." *O peuple heureux!* If you think about it, Klee was also ineligible due to his geographical coordinates: he wasn't from Lugano or environs. And then it must also be said, without intending any offense, that the newspaper had lots of other things to print.

To mention one, on June 30th, by beating Lucerne 4-0, Trello and Walaschek's Servette show themselves to be "abundantly deserving of the championship title of Swiss mobilization" and, to jump from one thing to another, is it or is it not necessary to report the news of an armed revolt "provoked" by Jewish "elements" in Galaz? (*Corriere del Ticino*, the "bel paese" where Paul Klee had just died). The Romanian Army had to intervene. Violent fighting in the streets. Over a hundred deaths mourned. Were mourned? By whom? Passive voice or adjectival participle? Or neither? In Lugano, where Klee would be cremated on July 1st, and in Locarno, where Klee died on June 29th, nobody was mourning over Galaz. In the beginning of July 1940 everyone was minding his or her own business and the dead in Galaz were no longer mourned due to the simple fact that they were dead: just like Paul Klee. Thus ended his duty toward his adopted country that had had such a hard time adopting him. General Guisan's order of the day, drawn up and delivered on June 27, 1940 and printed in the papers on July 2nd (precisely, one would say, to circumscribe something like an O around that June 29th, the day of Klee's passing) concluded merely by saying that "only death frees the Soldier from his duty towards his Country." Paul Klee could count himself among the liberated.

Since he wasn't exactly 100% one of us (even his death certificate lists Germany under "country of origin"), there was no fundamental reason to complain about the paper not announcing his death. On July 1st, the paper had to publish part thirty-eight of a serial novel by one of our writers, or print the fact that one of our fellow citizens, "getting out of bed (. . .) took a serious fall, breaking his leg. He was transported to the Civic Hospital by ambulance by our C.[roce] V.[erde] emergency services." Nor could one expect that in Bern Klee would get a monument in front of the Federal Building or in Bubenbergplatz (so-called in tribute to Adrian von Bubenberg, a great leader from a great past) as was done for Leonardo da Vinci near La Scala. Klee considered himself an alchemist at best, just as the viticulturist who makes wine is an alchemist (Paracelsus's word!), as is the baker who makes bread. If a soccer player had died—a Vernati, for example, a great traditional halfback, who also had the name of a great star, Sirio (Sirius)—it would have been another story, because soccer, in the hearts of simple people, is comparable to music, money, and mathematics, the three Ms that are universal languages. Music shares with money the intelligence of rhythm and in the same spirit, on the mathematical level, the precision of its calculations. Exchange is made primordial and if a traditional halfback or forward doesn't feel it, he doesn't become a halfback or a forward. The magic moment is rapidly changing the means into the end: scoring. Making a goal. And, as was put so well by Monsieur Philippe, discoursing on sports from St. Augustine to our Olympic games, apparently toward the end of the nineteenth century people realized that, for a myriad of reasons, money couldn't explain everything. Thus it became necessary to bring back into the system the body, beauty, enthusiasm for physical exertion, hygiene, honor, loyalty, chivalry.

What did Klee think?

Klee didn't think anything anymore because on July 2, 1940 he was making the trip from the crematory in Lugano to his "resting place" in Locarno-Muralto. Tuesday, July 2nd was the day of the V.(irgin) M.(ary)'s Visitation. The sun (this is in the paper, not the *National Zeitung* but the *Corriere del Ticino*, since Lugano and Locarno are in Ticino) rises at 4:33, sets at 8:26. Temperature at seven in the morning (Klee had come out of his death throes): 19° C. Idem, low of 14°. On this day in history: 1714, composer Cristoph Gluck was born. But just two days later the newspaper reported: "We've hit summer, you'll notice muggy heat in upcoming days; but it looks like there will be a repeat of last year's rainy summer, with periodic storms: at 8 A.M. in the city it was raining."

Thus July 2nd was a typical July day, and it seemed impossible that elsewhere the air was entirely toxic. In Paris for example. In Vienna the poison had long impregnated people's clothes, seeped into their hair, stuck to the soles of their shoes, coated the leaves of the trees in the boulevards, soiled the waters of the Danube. Someone would eat a sausage and he'd also consume a quantity of poison that would corrode his colon and make him pass blood; he'd take a few swigs of beer and have a strip of foam containing that poison on his mustache; this is why Sindelar, all other possibilities excluded, chose the gas valve. Without a plume, a thin layer, of smoke. Yet nobody noticed the slender trail of smoke going up (is there?) into the heavens (the heavens?) from the roof of the Lugano crematory on July 1, 1940. It was Klee's smoke, because Paul Klee was dead.

The man who came from Locarno to Lugano, on commission, to collect Klee's ashes, didn't have much difficulty finding the cemetery. But once he was inside, after parking his van by the fence, the paths that cut through the rectangles occupied by graves with so many big funerary monuments testifying to the Helvetic power of the patrician families of Lugano seemed as long as an Easter Mass, including the entire "Passio," which never seems to end. He heard the singular sound of the tiny bits of gravel under shoes: his. Finally the man, who wasn't sure he was going the right way to the crematory, heard a sound like a rake on gravel. It was an old groundskeeper whose face had taken on something of the weighty look of the faces effigied on the gravestones. With a slow, almost professorial wave of the arm, he indicated the path, but called the visitor back a second later. He said that the door might be closed, that he should try the side.

So it was. The crematory director listened with religious attention, as he was wont to do, then he took out a form and gave it to the man to sign. And while the director went into the other room, the delivery man, more to pass the time than to figure out what he was signing, read the words that had been penned in response to the printed questions.

Surname: Klee
Name: Paul
Religious denomination: Prot.
Profession: teacher
Country of origin: Germany
Most recent place of residence: Bern
Place of death: Muralto

Date of birth: 1879

Date of death: 29.VI.1940

1. When is cremation scheduled?   Date: 7/1/40
   Specific time: 16:30
2. Does the body need to be collected at the station? no
3. Would you like undertakers at the station? no
4. Will you be delivering the body to the crematory? yes
5. Will there be any eulogies at the ceremony? no
6. Would you like organ accompaniment? no
7. Would you like a floral decoration in the ceremony room? Selection I, II, III? (a straight horizontal line crossed out I, II, and III)
8. What do you intend to do with the remains? pick them up
9. Is the deceased a member of the Ticino Cremation Association? no. No. of shares: (diagonal dash in pen, at about a 30% incline)
10. To whom should the receipt be addressed? Rossi, Cesare, Locarno.

This form, duly completed and signed, must be immediately sent to TURBA, LUIGI (Gas Co.), Lugano.

City and date: Lugano, 7/1/1940

Signature: Cesare Rossi

This was followed by instructions, the list of fees. No Bach, no Mozart, nothing . . . what would Klee have chosen for himself? What key was he? B minor?

When the director reappeared at the door to that sort of sacristy (he looked like—how can I describe it?—like Louis Jouvet meets Buster Keaton, whom he, Cesare Rossi, at the cinema, tried to never miss), he was holding a kind of amphora, blue-gray in color. It was actually a terracotta jar, the kind they use in the country to store fresh butter for the winter. Buster Keaton led Cesare Rossi to the side door. His "good day" was a slight nod of the head. Right away, without making a sound, he closed the door.

Retracing the same route, between the big patrician family crypts, the delivery man (though now we know his name is Cesare Rossi) carried the jar with both hands nice and tight by the handles. But he was awkward, like at a baptism when they place that puffball of a child or grandchild in the hands of a clumsy father, a construction worker, say, and it seems like it would take no more than a breath to blow the baby out, to break his little bones. Thus Cesare Rossi, carrying Klee's ashes, couldn't even nod at the old man who had stopped raking the gravel and was watching him pass by.

He had to watch his step. It's easy, these days, to trip, to bump into things. The urn would have shattered and the ashes would have scattered over the gravel path and that would be that, it'd be out of his hands!

No, the long walk to the van in front of the cemetery went off without incident. The man set the urn on the sidewalk next to the rear tire with the utmost care, and opened the back door. But he hadn't thought to bring something to secure the urn. Clearly and audibly he said to himself: Idiot! He couldn't hold the urn between his knees like a milker in the Alps holds the pail into which he milks. He needed his legs to drive. And with the curves on the Monte Ceneri pass, the urn could slide back and forth like the plates and bowls in that Charlie Chaplin movie, hit the door and break into little pieces: farewell, my country, farewell.

The man thought enviously of army trucks with soldiers sitting squeezed together on low wooden benches. One of them could even fall asleep, but with his helmet on and a fellow soldier on both sides, he could snooze the entire trip away without any worry. He also thought, again with envy, of the trucks of potatoes from the Honorable Traugott Wahlen's plan—divine providence kept them all up, each supporting the other; not even the tiniest potato would suffer a bruise or anything of the sort.

But providence also provided for him, Mr. Cesare Rossi. In fact, he was standing there lost in thought when a young woman, perhaps mistaking him for a truck driver, came over: to ask him, well what do you know!, if the station was very far, because she needed to go to Locarno.

– To Locarno? Mr. Cesare Rossi asked, with visible happiness.

– Yes, to Locarno, the girl said, with a flash of suspicion in her eyes.

– Then come with me. In the amount of time it would take you to get to the station I'll have you in Locarno fresh as a rose, without having to transfer here or there, faster than express delivery. But you have to do something for me. You have to hold this jar.

The girl's hesitation lasted less than half a second, and not because of the business about the jar. The delivery man was still a stranger, but after all, these were not times to be too fussy, and not a day went by that her grandfather didn't say "à la guerre comme à la guerre!" Immediately, in a polite voice, she said: – Thank you! She could see right away that he was of a different sort compared to the many truck drivers she'd heard about who only drive with their left hand whereas, with their right, if you yield an inch, well, you'll end up in the meadow. Pigs. This guy, on the other hand, was a decent sort. He drove carefully, keeping his eyes on the wet road, more than even a student driver would, and every so often swore under his breath at a big pothole he hadn't been able to avoid—the road was a mess in certain spots, but after all, it was wartime and one can't have everything. Before they were even outside Lugano, he said to her:

– Good thing you're here!

– Me?

– Yes, because of the jar.

The jar, a kilo, a kilo and a half, jostled a little on her thighs, in the girl's hands, who held it as if she were holding a baby.

– Don't be scared if I tell you what's in there. There's a man's ashes in there.

The urn almost slipped out of her hands, almost rolled who knows where, to break, to shatter into a million pieces. But on instinct—because she felt like it was not a jar, not an urn, as if her entire womb, still untouched, could feel it—she gripped the urn tighter with both hands.

After a while the man continued:

– They're a painter's ashes, but I don't know anything about art–you?

– Art? I saw the *Mona Lisa* once, but not actually in real life. I've seen lots of ex-votos, I don't know, is that art?

– This one was a German, but not one of the crazy kind who used to come to Ascona, to Monte Verità. They all went around naked.

Now, however, it was no longer the era of the naked Germans. The Germans had entered Paris armored to the hilt. As for us, the Swiss, it was like the times when that tourist from Prague, Franz Kafka, toured our country, and was struck, especially in Lucerne, by the presence of so many soldiers, and in his diary wrote about his fear that their rifles would start firing.

There's always a lot of soldiers in Switzerland, so you can imagine what it would be like on a day like July 2, 1940, even if France's rapid collapse had made the authorities relax a little. It still wasn't the time to throw down one's arms and sing of victory "like the blackbird with a little good weather" as Father Dante says, and in fact, the majority of able men in town were crammed into jeeps, helmet to helmet, or were at barracks practicing port arms or running drills, or in the yards in front of the schools eating their ready-meals, or inside bunkers dusting the mouths of cannons, or picking up, with the tips of their bayonets, the paper tossed away by the sowers of discord: the thousand things, in short, that a Swiss soldier does during mobilization. This is why, on the sloping fields south of Ceneri, and especially in the Magadino plain towards Locarno, many women were working. And the car carrying Klee's ashes crossed Monte Ceneri without a single hitch. That good girl was really a good girl—she held the urn with both hands without allowing herself a break, without letting her back rest against the seat; she held her torso erect like the bathingsuited girls who carry the velvet-lined case with the Olympic medals, gold, silver, and bronze, at the Olympics.

They tilled the land, bent over heads of lettuce, those humbly-dressed women. The day was turning dark, with a sky that promised rain at any moment, but the women wouldn't stop pulling the weeds from row to row until the first little drops fell, making everyone run under the ledges of the sheds and barns, because in a second it'd be raining buckets. But no one thought that such a dark sky on a day like that was, all things considered, the sky in mourning, since no newspaper in the area had devoted a line to Klee's death.

No, it wasn't vacation time. For no one, much less for the internees. They certainly weren't left to collect mold in barracks or internment camps: the Poles were all or almost all strapping young men, as the girl holding the urn with Paul Klee's ashes on her thighs agreed—a cousin of hers, actually, having gone for the day to visit relatives up in a little town within the National Redoubt, laid her eyes on of one of those Poles, because he was holding a plow or taking a horse by the reins with gestures so noble that he must have belonged to the fallen Warsavian nobility; but the next day, they had already transferred the Pole to another town, perhaps even in the Val Blenio, and not to buy a sack of chestnuts for me, or for you, or for that old woman who's about to die, as one of our kids' songs goes. This cousin, a seventeen year old named Ermengarda, after seeing that Pole, never got her eyes back again.

It's infinite, the number of things that war does, thought the driver: indeed, it was as if there on the windshield, in two swipes of the wipers, someone had drawn the profile of a blond Pole, his hands, and the eyes of this Ermengarda, and despite the wipers shooting back and forth, the image remained. If she, that unfortunate girl, was an Ermengarde of times past, surely she wouldn't have fallen for a Pole?

– I don't even know your name, said the driver to the girl holding the urn on her lap almost as if she were holding a baby, so that it wouldn't hit the soft spot on its head against the windshield if they suddenly had to brake. Without taking her eyes off the Via Stradonino, since they were coming up on the turn for Locarno, she spoke.

– Giulia, the girl said. Giulia Sismondi.

– That's a very nice name you have.

He said these words very slowly, with a slowness that was perhaps awkward, yet full of the soft tranquility that mountain women have when they sing "Kyrie eleison" or "Causa nostrae laetitiae" or "Vas insignae devotionis": – . . . you have! he said, as if to mirror the van's soft stop with the slowness of his voice—no, the ashes inside that urn wouldn't suffer any disturbance: actually, if those ashes, for a few minutes, could have returned to life, recomposed into an intellect and a hand that obeyed this intellect, they would have sketched out a perfect drawing of an angel for that Giulia Sismondi. Who said:

– And you?

The driver, having shifted harmoniously from first to second gear, barely taking his eyes off the steering wheel and wagging his index finger back and forth like the windshield wipers, replied:

– Unh-uh, I don't want to be cremated.

– No, I meant your name.

– Oh, that, Cesare, my name's Cesare, Cesare Rossi. But I mean, I don't think I'll ever change my mind, I don't want to be cremated. If things get so bad for me that I don't even have my Sunday best to be buried in, they can go ahead and wrap me in a sheet.

Or I'll do it like Fulberta from Val Canaria, who dressed her dead husband in his army uniform and kept on saying to everyone who came over that he'd loved being a soldier so much, he really loved it. In a sheet, in my wedding clothes, I'm going to have them put me in a casket, same as people have always done. Whereas the Germans . . .

Miss Giulia Sismondi pressed on the urn a little as if she were pressing down on the painter's head, almost as if he were about to have an operation without anesthesia and she had been asked to act as a kind of aide, to keep his head still, like a dental assistant—yes, if those ashes, for an instant, could have come back to life, Klee would have certainly drawn for her, in two lines, without her knowing, a bird of paradise, its trill cutting through the air.

As they approached Locarno and the houses were closer together—a kid could pop out from any side street without warning, and then there was a group of cyclists in gray-green with helmets on and rifles slung over their shoulders—Cesare Rossi turned all of his concentration to driving the van. After a while, never taking his eyes off the road, he said that they were going to bring the urn where it needed to go and then he would leave her at Piazza Grande or wherever was convenient for her, but first he wanted to stop for a few minutes to have a drink together, it would really be a pleasure—he really didn't know how he would have done it alone, with that jar.

And if . . . If *Der Schöpfer*, *Le créateur*, *The Creator* (1934), coming out of its 42 x 53.5 square and flapping its wings like an owl, all crimson, with feet that look like flippers, over the Swiss territory of Locarno, if the god of creation, of the big bang, decided to make one of the tires blow? Or by pouring a puddle of oil on a half-curve, as the gods of the past used to do when on a divine whim or with good reason they willed a mortal's downfall, made the van crash into a wall so that the urn would break into a hundred pieces . . . ? Couldn't, from the scattering ashes, a piece of that ash, still almost warm, make its way into Giulia Sismondi's vulva-urn and grow there? The natural humors of the chaste virgin would have brought life to that spermatozoon of this lone miracle: like a glob of condensed milk, a piece of ice, falling into a drop of warm water . . . Couldn't Klee's Creator bring Klee back to life by fertilizing the girl who carried the painter's ashes in her lap?

But that dear girl didn't ask herself absurd complicated questions. She concentrated on holding the urn tight on her lap with its China-blue friezes on grayish-blue. Only one question crossed her mind: how come Signor Cesare Rossi wasn't at one of the hundred thousand posts guarding the border but instead going around transporting the ashes of, to put it bluntly, Lutherans, from the crematory to who knows where? It would have been simple, she could have just asked, but it seemed indelicate. And? And if he had responded: I only have one lung, I have a heart murmur, I have a herniatied disc, I have tuberculosis: You name it, Miss Health Officer. Insufficient height couldn't have been the culprit (our nation, like all self-respecting countries, doesn't want an army of dwarves, of rachitic chimney-sweeps, it's not the Circus Knie) because Rossi was definitely much taller than the 1.56 meters that get you rejected. Or was it 1.58? Or was it because of flat feet? The army turns away the flat-footed, you know.

Giulia Sismondi's innocent green eyes, in harmonious unison, at the will of her Will, rolled down: the man had regular sandals, the kind you could trade for a cup of milk, or even less. If Giulia Sismondi could have seen a single drawing by the painter she was carrying in her lap (she handled it with careful fingers—proximal phalange, intermediate phalange, distal phalange, carpal, metacarpal, radius, ulna, humerus, clavicle, and then what—that urn with his ashes inside), why couldn't she imagine that painter pulling a random piece of paper, a random pencil stump (but, be careful, it might be sharp) out of his pocket and he, the creator, drawing blue, aristocratic sandals for a meticulous, attentive driver like this Cesare Rossi? Who was careful about the potholes at the crossroads: at the bottom of the Ceneri he'd blurted out "Damn this road" that required looking right and left ten times, enough to give you a neckache—and why didn't they put in a stoplight!—but for some reason she was absorbed in thoughts of Christ on the cross, and yes, it was long past Easter—it was the middle of summer, it was the 2nd of the month of July.

With sandals sketched by Klee, even a Cesare Rossi could have felt like a St. Peter walking on water with the protection and outstretched hand of Christ—

do déda via da tèra

—off the ground, that's what Angelo the sacristan said when a car, or a truck, stopped to pick him up on that dusty road: off the ground, with those sore feet Angelo had—yet he was singing a vesper divinely—it was heaven. Even Cesare Rossi, with those sandals sketched by Klee, could have walked on air like the eleven-man team of the Holy Sob (free-thinkers and freemasons, without a second thought, would have called them Heaven's Spew), all headwork, playing in the air:

Baruch

Balak   Zadoc

Adramelech   Moloch   Abimelech

Amalek   Habakkuk   Melchizedek   Walaschek   Enoch

– Oh no, f***!—Absalom the Beautiful, in extremis, at the edge of the penalty area, miraculously managed to censor himself after the first letter; even if in heaven, after the Archangel Michael, they're loath to use red cards. – No! And Achitophel wasn't about to go back on his bad advice, but in heaven, ever since Lucifer's times, they tend to let certain things in the eastern ear and out the western ear! Absalom and Achitophel not even considered worthy of the bench, in favor of Sanballat, Abinadab, those two old bumblers! Not even Habakkuk was listening—he was praying for God to make his feet like deer hooves so he could climb steep mountains. Baruch, however, was shaking his head—is it or is it not 1940?—and the wrath of God has brought great misfortune upon us, reducing man to eating the flesh of his own sons and daughters. Even if the lake was completely calm, and a fisherman on his boat asked for the proper silence: Cesare Rossi's van had reached the end of its trip. One could hear the clear sound of crickets and cicadas in the fields and the vineyards sloping up to the hills and mountains. Stopping in front of a gate, the driver got out and then took the urn with the ashes from the girl's hands and brought it to Paul Klee's widow, then went back to get the folder with the documentation: the death confirmation, the death certificate, the record from the crematory, the receipt from the Ticinese Cremation Association, Lugano, on which "the undersigned confirms having personally received the ashes of the deceased Klee Paolo, cremated and released to the Committee. In testimony whereof, Cesare Rossi."

That was it. Cesare Rossi then decided, on the way to Piazza Grande, not to go to Canetti's, a wineseller who was also an inspired center forward, an expert in dribbling close to the goal, since it didn't seem like a time for wine. They decided to go to Planzi's for frappés, and chatted about their lives for ten minutes or so. The girl was so fully intent on what the man was saying, fully absorbed in saying yes, she understood, he was right, he'd done the right thing, that she didn't see a miniscule spider, an almost microscopic little dot, moving across the marble table a centimeter away from her glass. Not seeing it, she didn't have the temptation to crush it, she didn't wonder things like: what does your glass look like to it? A wandering rock? What about your pinky? One of the enormous highly mobile proboscises of the monstrous saurian that you are? That spider, which takes up no more space than a ground of finely ground coffee, does it have a heart, a sex, a nervous system, what atomic dose of fear could it endure? Klee couldn't have come to its defense in a world that crushed everything; he would never again depict its right to life, because now Klee was dead. And not even by continuing to develop all the techniques he had made his own and redoubling the frenzied activity of his last months could he have again represented the archeology, the epiphany, the growth and the death of one of the countless leaves that, in spite of Hitler and other obscenities, had bloomed in that 1940 spring: the delicate leaf of a tree, of a flower, that brightens the lives of the birds of God, the flower that blooms again every spring—because Klee would never bloom again. He was dead. And dead along with him, it seemed, now that the beasts of the Generalstaben in Berlin and other capitals were winning, were the cats with their backs made of elastic elasticity, kittens that curl up imploringly, lambs that can trot on grass without trampling it, kitties that sleep with their delicate backs arched, fawns that can sense the ominous air, little ones of different stripes that have survived distant travels: the water-tower bird seemed hopelessly ensnared in the all-seeing eye of 1938; you can only ward off the gaze of the Medusa for so long, and certainly not—fetch Medusa, turn him into stone!—for eternity. Because Paul Klee was dead. And in a letter from April 6, 1978, Dr. Enrico Uehlinger writes despondently: "I asked around at the Sant'Agnese Clinic. Shamefully, I couldn't find anything of note in the archives, the administrative records, or lab records: date of admittance, death, results of a urine analysis, no description of the illness or the cause of death, which from the literature appears to have been scleroderma. The attending clinicians are dead, the old sister-nurses I consulted only vaguely remembered Klee and his wife Lily who came with him. No one can give me specific information, but it's possible that the relevant documents were given to other scholars—there's been mention of a Japanese . . . I'm so sorry (. . .)."

And Walaschek?

It was Snoozy's granddaughter who jumped up, all red and white in the face, all Swiss, all the colors of our flag, just like Carl Spitteler wanted, and also, all infuriated. She was also mad at Scribe O/17360, chosen—perhaps she didn't know—by *Wille*, and who, moreover, had been silent for more than an academic hour, that is, for over forty-five minutes.

– You be quiet, she shouted at the scribe. Be quiet, with those beat-up priest shoes, your black priest raincoat, your priest hat, your priest crewneck. If I had a machine gun I'd kill all the priests and professors like you. Professor of Bullshit!

A juvenile titter broke out in the crowd. The bike repairman nudged the baker, hissing in his ear:

– Don't say anything, that's not really what he's called, it's just a generic nickname.

Snoozy's granddaughter wasn't backing down:

– What about Walaschek?

One never knows from what deep places, for what cause, hiding in a fold of the intestines, from what scrotum, what ulcer or open sore, comes the hate, so diffuse in the world, which is concentrated within the rings of stadiums.

– Hmpf, goddamned referee.

According to Snoozy's granddaughter, no one should let a family man be a teacher and a referee. It ruins everything, she said: the game, school, and family, all at the same time. Big-talking windbags who stink to high heaven, they should wipe some of the dust off of their eyes. Screw-ups at home and phonies at school, bigmouth layabouts with their completely ridiculous black shorts clinging to their bums and their tight black jackets sanctimoniously buttoned up with those little whistles in their mouths. Hmpf.

The whistlers in the stadium put their four fingers in their mouths and the entire area around the stadium, for a good distance of streets and streetcorners, filled up with whistles of disapproval.

Scribe O/17360 looked at that insolent granddaughter of Snoozy's with no sympathy whatsoever. Potato-popping moron in G major, as useless as an apple that falls off the tree too soon. She thinks she can come here and lay down the law. But no more is it the era of the bailiffs nor the times of the strong and free Swiss, who are also, as says the great Francesco, savage and rustic by nature: a horrid, ignorant people. There was nothing to get so worked up about, Walaschek was going back home, unlike Klee on July 2, 1940, in a little terracotta jar—he was in first class on the Bern-Geneva InterCity train. They'd been in Bern celebrating, fifty years later, in honor of that old fox Rappan, inventor of the "bolt"—and how many great memories they shared. The photo display up in the hall, with a big white-crossed red flag behind it that would also have pleased Carl Spitteler, didn't show Minelli, the captain, great pillar of the defense. And the others? Where is Trello, who died near the end of the war; where Ramseyer, so long ago, and with a name that seemed to belong to the age of the pharaohs; where Pulver, where . . .? And Vernati, the traditional halfback with the name of a great star—Sirio—was the only one wearing a wool vest under his jacket. He must have had a wife who doled out advice fourteen hours out of twenty-four: bundle up! The days when he had to cover the entire midfield and set up his outside forwards were over. Now he too could let loose a little: *pinta trahit pintam trahit altera pintula pintam*: one pint leads to another.

Georges Aeby, Walaschek's outside left, had his eyes closed too. Once in a while he let out a light snore. They had both decided to catch a little shuteye, without a word, as if they were still twenty and on the train home at night, with their shins beat up by the opposing defenders, and dog tired, perhaps too with the bitter taste of defeat and the not so appealing prospect of Monday.

What was Georges Aeby thinking, there opposite him? Every so often their knees bumped, or their feet. On his home field, at Charmilles, but also at the Wankdorf as on April 18, 1938, but also at the Parc des Princes in Paris, as against the German white team, but also at the Prater in Vienna, they could play with their eyes closed. Walaschek would meet him again, feinting first with the easy movements of a girl spinning a Hula-Hoop around her unripe hips, and then with a precise tap with the outside of his foot. He knew how and when he would break free, where to pass in order to have a clear shot toward the goal. There, when the center arrives, vigor and grace must converge. There, as one great master of technique (de Caussade) says, what grace achieves in this state of simplicity is always a source of wonder for watchful eyes and enlightened minds. Without method, yet most exact; without rule, yet most orderly; without reflection, yet most profound; without skill, yet thoroughly well-constructed, without effort, yet accomplishing everything; and without foresight, yet nothing could be better suited to unexpected events.

The train conductor (was he really a conductor, or was he a mystic who wanted to explain to the travelers—especially Walaschek—the meaning of Klee's alphabet? Was it just a ruse, his punching the ticket—a little round circle, or rather, a little oval, like Klee's O over Walaschek's name, which obliterates the Wala, in the *National Zeitung* from that very remote April 19, 1938—so that he could deliver his speech? In truth, he whispered with a breath, it's completely useless for man to get upset—everything that happens in him is like a dream: one shadow chases and destroys another, chimeras keep coming and coming in those who sleep, some that disturb, others that console; the soul is the plaything of these phantoms that devour one another, and waking only demonstrates that there's nothing that can stop them), the train conductor hadn't recognized them: neither the outside left, who was very lightly, almost imperceptibly snoring, nor the inside forward, so contentedly dreaming comforting things. They could be any pair of Genevans coming back from Bern, tired from a business meeting. "Tired but happy," as kids might write in school compositions. Still not retired at that age? Maybe they had a private family business?

Just past Laussane, Walaschek was transported into another dream, less brief this time (also because Aeby, now awake, was being careful not to hit him with his knee like before—how he'd apologized!). First he dreamed of a stadium like the one in Cologne—maybe it was Cologne, because it was all a-flutter with swastika flags and packs of officers and soldiers were stationed at the entrances and in various parts of the stadium—but then instead of heading for the sixteen-meter line, he found himself dribbling the ball down a mountain road after a sudden heavy snowfall in early March, the trees loaded with snow, the wind kicking up all of a sudden, sweeping away the black clouds and opening the path of the sun; and every so often a gust of wind, stirring larches and firs, raised a cloud of snow, a dense ball of powder, and the whole sun lit up, blinding, the geometric light guiding his dribble, with Walaschek waving his arms like a priest incensing the altar, maybe at St. Peter's? Or the Pope on Easter morning? And candles flickered like the icicles hanging from a tin roof up in the mountains that a little boy knocked with his ski pole, tinkling like a harpsichord as they fell: he had the impression of breaking into flight with the doves over a bay near Oslo, Switzerland-Norway, an all-blue sky just barely dotted with little white clouds like balls of cotton, like little armchairs for royal princesses.

After a while, not a living soul was to be seen, there were no more whistles or applause, and then he noticed that it wasn't Cologne or Oslo, it was the rough field on the outskirts of Geneva where he used to meet up with his friends. It was a classic national team: six from the Grasshoppers, four from Servette, one from Lugano; Switzerland made its entrance onto the field to greet both the officials and the crowd as the band played the national anthem with an enthusiasm that hit you right in the thighs, then the solar plexus, then the throat, with the urge to sing along. In five minutes the sarabanda would begin and they'd have to dance. A footballer is like an improvisational actor: at the opening whistle he still doesn't know exactly what he's going to do, so much depends on the first few minutes, on the reaction of the crowd, on a hundred other things—that actor was right when he said that one of the best actors in the world was Falcao, the Brazilian—he too certainly needs a day of grace.

The white team had also lined up before the officials, extending their arms upward in the Nazi salute; eleven arms that seemed like so many cannon barrels. Walaschek half-swore; the first time he'd sworn at home, his grandmother Jenny Morel dropped her cup of bread soaking in milk. It all ended up on the floor in a big puddle.

But then he dreamed that a girl was coming directly toward him from one of the little hills in the surrounding terrain, toward him in his classic position as inside forward, at that moment back supporting the defense, trying to get control of the ball. She was carrying a garland of flowers. It wasn't one of those oval garlands for funerals: it was one of those lovely, light, fresh ones, the kind we don't have, the leis that Hawaiians put around the neck of a guest of honor, a great man, a star. He bowed so that the girl didn't have to bend down to crown him. The garland split him in half, Wala on one side, Schek on the other. That painter from Bern didn't put the girl in his painting, but the girl is there, alive. Perhaps it's the younger sister or the cousin of the girl Pindar talks about, so determined, for her hero, to slacken the bridles of her virginity.

Then Walaschek noticed that it wasn't really a garland but a wide sash, the *ruban vert* that divides the chest diagonally, which is still used in certain pageants, placed around the beautiful bodies of the most beautiful people in the world; and then he returned to the circle in midfield, just in time to go after a high pass that was flying right toward him. He controlled it with a *sophia* that would have delighted a Greek, and with two dribbles, pretending to retreat, freed himself from an opponent on the same diagonal, like a bishop in check with a king or queen. Walaschek then stood erect with the majesty of the king in *Überschach, The Great Chess Game,* 1937.

Then he turned.

He turned like that émigré Klee turning to look at what there was to see in 1939. Still dribbling the ball, he sped toward the opponents' penalty box, where he could see and hear the throng of ally jerseys and enemy jerseys. Moving forward, you have to keep an eye on everything, like a poet, a painter, a composer: from the first syllable to the last, from white to black, from the first note to the finale. Klee's O was only the beginning of his invocation, his dream: O gams, gams go! O iambs, iambs go. Yellow, if you wish, like Van Gogh, the blue of Vermeer, the black of Rembrandt and Klee. At the rhythm, if you wish, of anapests, of false three-quarters, a Stravinsky who "samples" from Pergolesi. He feinted a move toward the sideline, toward the corner; he imitated the soft bow of the willow, of the alder, of heron wings in the air, in the wind, of silk, of flanks without weight. Legs, muddle the minds of those pitbull fullbacks, those butcher halfbacks who slide into your ankles and swear they're going for the ball, throw them on their backs with your scanzontic rhythm, alternate imagination and ingenuity to confuse every command post, the tyrants deaf-mute to life—to life. Even an inside forward, like a dancer, has to free the rhythms of the body patiently trained with freedom and discipline. If after your pass the outside runs along the sidelines, taps the ball, and then aims right into the sixteen-meter zone, then you—white, color of the miracle—you jump, trying to stay up as long as you can. Then, never losing

sight of the trajectory of the ball as it soars, calculating the timing in infinitesimal divisions with mathematical brainwork, turn
your head to the left, tense your neck. For an instant you'll feel
what it's like to levitate like saints do during miracles, in what
they say is a violation of physical laws, transgressing them in a
total sublimation of yourself, in ecstasy. When the ball, soaring,
crosses to you, all the ecstasy will transform into energy for your
muscles, into drive for your neck and spine. Your head will rotate
with violence and precision, between sixty and ninety degrees,
striking the ball with your right temple, as if it were the tip of a
triangle, the other points being Georges Aeby's foot and the top
net-corner to the goalkeeper's right: that is, if the event will come
to its epiphany.

Advancing toward the penalty box, then, he kept an eye on
Georges Aeby who always seemed to be snoozing but in fact was
as agile as a cat. Or Belli might make a downfield pass: an inside forward's work is analogous to the mental labor of a great
chess master in simultaneous play, in blitz matches—he was
unpredictable, Belli, who roved on slightly bowed legs outside
the box; who looked, from high up in the stands, like a toddler
distracted by something or other, dragging around a kilometer's
worth of snacks in his nappies, whereas he was actually trying to
avoid the offside, and he pounced for the deep pass like a cat in
the bushes out in the countryside—like a rocket. With the genial
Sindelar always in his mind's eye. With them—Klee said—he'd
invent a quadrilateral as a sign for rotation, for the movement of
the vertical-horizontal symbol: a dynamo, an X, a rotating cross.
Thus he headed for the opponent's penalty box, dodging and not

neglecting to set up the left for the big kick, in which he would impart all the rage of 1938. He knows that an enemy is at his heels—ready, if he catches him, to grab him by the shirt, jerk him back and pull him down.

People are coming with whom I must not be.

He knew he was caught between two fires. He took three more steps, right, left, right, and then his energy and intelligence would be unleashed upon the left: one, two, three,

and off he raced,
like one of those who at Verona run,
to gain the mantle green; and he appeared
no loser, but like one who has already won.

TRANSLATOR'S NOTES

The purpose of these notes is not to provide the reader with a complete bibliography and glossary, but merely with an informal guide to some of the quotations and references (literary, historical, geographical, sportive, and of course Helvetian) utilized by the author in composing his Dream, *and by the translator in preparing this English-language edition.*

The translators of published works quoted here have only been named where necessary to avoid confusion between multiple editions of extant translations.

—Ed.

p. 3   *Pardon, gentles all, etc.*: translator's epigraphs, included with the complicity of the author.

p. 7   *a Russian said*: Joseph Brodsky, "In a Room and a Half," *Less than One*, p. 467.

p. 7   *"I shall show you some cases . . . The individual pattern . . ."*: Paul Klee, *Notebooks Volume 2: The Nature of Nature*, Ed. Jürg Spiller, Trans. Heinz Norden, p. 183, 185.

p. 9   *Traugott Wahlen*: Friedrich Traugott Wahlen (1899–1985), politician and head of the Swiss Federal Office for War Nourishment, who instituted a plan to cultivate all available patches of land, thereby averting famine and increasing Switzerland's self-sufficiency.

p. 10   *the National Redoubt*: the Swiss National Redoubt was a defensive plan consisting of multiple fortress complexes barring passage through the Alps, developed during World War II to defend against a possible German invasion.

p. 10   *Dinamo Ossasco*: Djalma Santos (1929–), legendary Brazilian right-back in the '50s and '60s; Nilton Santos (1925–), Brazilian left-back from the '40s to the '60s; and other Brazilian players alongside "local" characters.

p. 10   *General Guisan*: Henri Guisan (1874–1960), General of the Swiss Army during World War II, is best remembered for effectively mobilizing the Swiss to prepare for resistance against a possible invasion by Nazi Germany in 1940.

p. 11   *Dopolavoro*: abbreviation for Opera Nazionale Dopolavoro (OND), or National Recreation Club, a leisure and sports association for workers established by the Fascist regime.

p. 12   *oriundi*: immigrants of native ancestry, which has historically qualified many football players to be allowed onto Swiss teams.

p. 12   *Brianza*: an area in Lombardy, Italy, just below the Swiss border.

p. 14   "*. . . been writ so quick*": Dante, *Inferno* XXIV.100, Trans. Robert and Jean Hollander.

p. 14   "*My tragedy is finished . . .*": attributed to Racine.

p. 14   "*language no longer known*": Giovanni Pascoli, "Addio."

p. 14   *The song of the birds*, etc.: ibid.

p. 14   "*But tell me . . .*": *Letters of Vincent Van Gogh*, Trans. Mark Roskill, pp. 240–1.

p. 15   *Johanna Trosiener*: Johanna Schopenhauer, née Trosiener (1766–1838), Arthur Schopenhauer's mother.

p. 15   *il pleure dans mon coeur . . .*: Paul Verlaine, "Il pleure dans mon coeur." (It weeps in my heart AS it rains on the city).

p. 15   *"Bagnacaval does well to have no sons"*: Dante, *Purgatory* XIV.115, Trans. Mark Musa.

p. 18   *Thus spake Zolla*: reference to *Archetypes* (1981) by Elémire Zolla (1926–2002), writer, critic, and professor of Anglo-American literature at Rome's La Sapienza.

p. 19   *Ranuccio Bianchi Bandinelli*: Ranuccio Bianchi Bandinelli (1900–1975), Italian anti-fascist archeologist and art historian.

p. 19   *curved lines . . . are charged with a unique sensitivity*: Ranuccio Bianchi Bandinelli, *Dal diario di un borghese e altri scritti*, p. 316.

p. 20   *tuba mirum spargens . . .*: from the "Dies Irae": "The trumpet scatters a wondrous sound / throughout the [deserts] all around."

p. 21   *in groups of ten, twenty, four, seven, eight*: *Orlando Furioso*, IX. 3, Trans. Guido Walkman.

p. 22   *lama sabachthani*: Aramaic; in Matthew 27 and Mark 15 as: "Why hast Thou forsaken Me?"

p. 24   *erased above the waist*: reference to Dante, *Inferno* X.33, "da la cintola in sù tutto 'l vedrai."

p. 24   *squat like a sparrowhawk just alighted from its perch*: as in Klee's *Creator* (*Der Schöpfer*), 1934.

p. 24   *Masaryk and Beneš*: Tomáš Garrigue Masaryk (1850–1937), founder and first president of Czechoslovakia; Edvard Beneš (1884–1948), leader of the Czechoslovak independence movement and the second president of Czechoslovakia.

p. 24   *. . . from the waist down*: Dante, *Inferno* X.33, modified from: "you can see all of him from the waist up." Trans. Jean and Robert Hollander.

p. 24   *a certain boy from the mountains*: that is, the author himself.

p. 25   *föhn*: a warm, dry wind that blows down a mountain range, especially the northern slopes of the Alps.

p. 25   *the place, the time, the seed of their begetting and their birth*: Dante, *Inferno* III.104–5. Trans. Robert and Jean Hollander.

p. 27   *Sepp Herberger*: Josef "Sepp" Herberger (1897–1977), German soccer player and manager in the '30s (the *Reichsfußballtrainer*) and then coach in the '50s–'60s; a renowned strategist of the game who rebuilt German football after the war.

p. 32   *our great Gottfried*: Gottfried Keller (1819–1890), nineteenth century Swiss novelist.

p. 35   *Shklovsky*: quotations from *A Sentimental Journey*, pp. 145, 276, 110.

p. 36   *During the Revolution . . .*: Marina Tsvetaeva, *A Captive Spirit*, pp. 135, 72.

p. 36   *Switzerland won't let any Russians in . . .*: Marina Tsvetayeva, in *Letters, Summer 1926*, p. 110.

p. 38   *Peyroteo*: Fernando Baptista de Seixas Peyroteo (1918–1978).

p. 39   *Rhone, Rhine, Iber, Seine, Elbe, Loire, Ebro*: Petrarch, Sonnet 148. (All names of rivers.)

p. 39   *iahn swan puč*, et al.: soccer players with monosyllabic names: Antonín Puč, Ruud Krol, Helmut Rahn, Johan Cruyff, Mihály Tóth, etc.

p. 40   *Bacigalupo, Ballarin, Maroso*: Valerio Bacigalupo, Aldo Ballarin, Virgilio Maroso. Three of the players for Torino A.C. who died in the Superga airplane crash in 1949, which killed everyone aboard: most of the team, officials, journalists, and crew.

p. 40   goats "with Semitic faces": allusion to Umberto Saba's
         poem "La Capra" (The Goat).

p. 40   mi ritrovái | per una sélva | oscúra (I found myself in a
         dark wood): Dante, Inferno I.2.

p. 40   e per la sélva | a tutta bríglia | il cáccia (and [she] galloped
         full tilt through the forest): Ariosto, Orlando Furioso I.13.

p. 41   mi stringerá | per un pensiéro | il cuóre (and the thought
         will clutch my heart): Umberto Saba, "Quest'anno" (This
         Year).

p. 41   The word is the phallus of the spirit, centrally rooted: Gott-
         fried Benn, "Wort ist der Phallus des Geistes, zentral
         verwurzelt."

p. 41   Bacigalupo . . . Schiaffino: for the first three players, see note
         above; Otone, Avolio, Berlingiero, Avino are from Ariosto's
         Orlando Furioso; the last four are other footballers.

p. 43   Dimitrijević: Vladimir Dimitrijević, editor and founder
         of L'Âge d'Homme publishing house.

p. 43   Artimovics: Josef.

p. 44   Mazzini: Giuseppe Mazzini (1805–1872), Italian revo-
         lutionary who helped unify the country and who spent

time exiled in Grenchen in 1834. He was elected a citizen by the residents but eventually deported anyway.

p. 44   *"Our horizon has been darkly clouded . . ."*: *Psychoanalysis and Faith: The Letters of Sigmund Freud and Oskar Pfister*, p. 140.

p. 44   *Mr. Vuilleumier*: Marc Vuilleumier, contemporary Swiss historian, author of *Immigrants and Refugees In Switzerland*.

p. 45   *". . . no country would allow him to enter . . ."*: Ernest Jones, *The Life and Work of Sigmund Freud*, p. 501.

p. 45   *Joseph Roth*: Joseph Roth (1894–1939), Austrian journalist and novelist.

p. 46   *She stood at the entrance, her eyes full of tears . . .*: Nina Nikolaevna Berberova, *The Italics Are Mine*, p. 356.

p. 46   *"Each socket seemed a ring without a gem"*: Dante, *Purgatory* XXIII.31, Trans. Dorothy Sayers.

p. 47   *"And behold, one shade . . ."*: Dante, *Purgatory* XXIII.40–1, Trans. Robert Durling.

p. 48   *synderesis*: a term from medieval scholastic philosophy signifying the innate principle in the moral consciousness of all people that directs the agent to good and restrains him from evil.

p. 48   *"unbind for the hero the fair girdle of her virginity"*: *The Extant Odes of Pindar*, Trans. Ernest Myers, p. 168.

p. 48   *"one mustn't forget that all poets of the world have loved soldiers"*: cf. "Since time immemorial, the Russian poet has left glory to the military and paid homage to this glory." *Earthly Signs: Moscow Diaries 1917–1922*, p. 178.

p. 49   *they were incinerated some five years later*: Ernest Jones, *The Life and Work of Sigmund Freud*, Vol. III, p. 521.

p. 49   *the federal Foreigners' Police*: in 1917, an ordinance of the Federal Council of Switzerland established the Foreigners' Police as a branch of the Federal Department of Justice and Police to coordinate the cantons' surveillance of foreigners in wartime.

p. 50   *". . . Do you really think the Germans are unkind to the Jews?"*: Ernest Jones, *The Life and Work of Sigmund Freud, Volume III*, p. 515.

p. 51   *"The more horrible . . ."*: *The Diaries of Paul Klee, 1898–1918*, pp. 313, 315.

p. 51   *o, long and hoarse*: Dante, *Purgatory* V.27, Trans. Arthur John Butler.

p. 51   *I have long been of the opinion* . . .: Arthur Schopenhauer, *The World as Will and Idea*, Vol. 2, pp. 199, 198.

p. 55   *Lei* and *Voi*: of the two possible formal forms of address, the Fascists required the use of *Voi* over *Lei*, which was the standard at the time and has been since the end of the Fascist era.

p. 57   *Three times it turned her round with all the waters*: Dante, *Inferno* XXVI.139, Trans. Allen Mandelbaum.

p. 57   *"God is an intelligible sphere . . .": "Sermo de sphaera intelligibili"* (Discourse on the Intelligible Sphere).

p. 58   *Cheer up!* . . .: Paul Klee, "Creative Credo."

p. 60   *Manfredi in Purgatory*: Dante, *Purgatory* III.112.

p. 62   *half a million lire*: about €250 or $340.

p. 62   *Pierino Selmoni*: contemporary Swiss sculptor.

p. 63   *as Gide says about Poussin*: "It was by retaining and restoring tradition, when it was slipping away, that Poussin was able to seem to Delacroix healthily revolutionary." André Gide, *Autumn Leaves*, p. 177.

p. 63   *"immense horrible abyss"*: Giacomo Leopardi, "Canto Notturno," line 35.

p. 65   *Madamina! Il catalogo è questo*: Mozart, *Don Giovanni*.

p. 67   *Sir Bertrand of Wales*: alias Bertrand Russell.

p. 69   *Cantor's aleph-0*: Georg Cantor (1845–1918), German mathematician, who invented set theory, which demonstrates the "infinity of infinities." This was also seen as a challenge to God's role as the ultimate infinity. The Hebrew aleph was Cantor's designation for cardinal numbers, and omega for ordinals.

p. 71   *Père Jean-Pierre*: Jean-Pierre de Caussade (1675–1751), French Jesuit priest, known for his belief that the present moment is a sacrament from God.

p. 71   *Nuntio vobis gaudium magnum*: "I announce a great joy to you," a centuries-old locution used in the announcement of a new Pope (usually followed by: "Habemus Papam"— we have a Pope).

p. 74   *Fontana*: village in Ticino near Gotthard.

p. 75   *the Sicilian bull*: Ancient Greek torture device.

p. 76   *Sulla*: Lucius Cornelius Sulla (c. 138 BCE–78 BCE), Roman dictator notorious for executing presumed enemies of the state.

p. 77   *Zwingli*: Huldrych Zwingli (1484–1531), leader of the

Reformation in Switzerland.

p. 79   *Major Davel*: Major Jean Daniel Abraham Davel (1670–
         1723), soldier and patriot who led a rebellion to free Canton
         Vaud from the rule of Bern, for which he was executed.

p. 79   *Winkelried*: Arnold von Winkelried, legendary hero who
         brought about the victory of the Old Swiss Confederacy
         against the Hapsburg Army (in the 1386 Battle of Sem-
         pach) by throwing himself upon (or "embracing") the
         Austrian pikes and thus creating an opening through
         which the Swiss could attack.

p. 79   *"By gathering with a wide embrace . . ."*: William Words-
         worth, "The Church of San Salvador, Seen from the Lake
         of Lugano."

p. 79   *More grace than we asked for, St. Anthony!*: from an expres-
         sion indicating one has received more than was requested.

p. 80   *parva si licet*: "Si parva licet componere magnis" (if one
         may compare the small with the great), Virgil, *Georgics*
         4.176.

p. 80   *"Johnny of the Vine . . ."*: Swiss and Northern Italian proverb.

p. 81   *Ambrosiana to Internazionale*: Milan's team, Football
         Club Internazionale Milano, or "Inter," was renamed Am-

brosiana after the patron saint of Milan, Ambrose, during the Fascist era.

p. 83   *"Alcina drew the fishes to the shore . . .":* Orlando furioso., VI. 38, Trans. John Hoole.

p. 85   *It is the same everywhere . . .:* The Letters of Vincent Van Gogh, pp. 322–3.

p. 86   *You called, you shouted, you shattered my deafness!:* St. Augustine, *Confessions* X.27, Trans. Carolinne White.

p. 86   *"accident in substance":* Dante, *Vita Nuova* XXV.

p. 89   *libido dominandi:* "lust for domination," St. Augustine, *City of God.*

p. 90   *Bedoleto:* Bedretto, a municipality in the Ticino.

p. 91   *Ite missa est:* the dismissal formula that concludes the Roman Mass: "Go, the dismissal has been made."

p. 92   *St. Nicholas:* patron saint of Switzerland.

p. 92   *"Anyway . . . the color range . . .":* Letters of Vincent Van Gogh, p. 317.

p. 95   *Chi ha paura dell'uomo nero?:* who's afraid of the boogeyman? (literally: "black man").

p. 96   . . . *It is sweet, Helvetia, to die for you*: Swiss national anthem until 1961, known as "Ci chiami, o Patria" (Call Us, O Country) in Italian.

p. 100   . . . *you will still live, for all time, in my verse*: Ovid, *Tristia* VI.21–2, 35–6, Trans. A. S. Kline.

p. 100   *For if a man takes delight in toil and expenditure . . .*: Pindar, *The Complete Odes*, Trans. Anthony Verity.

p. 102   *the sound of his sighs*: Giorgio Orelli (b. 1921), *Il suono dei sospiri* (The Sound of Sighs, a monograph on Petrarch).

p. 102   *Susanna Orelli*: Swiss social worker and temperance activist (1845–1939).

p. 105   *Mortal aims befit mortal men*: Pindar, Isthmian V, Trans. John Sandys.

p. 105   *slapping his thigh like Dante's farmer*: Inferno XXIV.7–9.

p. 105   *But the ancient splendor sleeps*: Pindar, Isthmian VII, Trans. William Race.

p. 107   *Io tengo una pistola . . .*: "I've got a loaded gun . . . " "I've got six brothers, their eyes are black and white, I've got six brothers, they'll murder you. From "La mamma di Rosina," Italian folk song.

p. 107   *dixit Caesar, in Rome after the Rubicon*: Plutarch, *Life of Caesar*, 35.

p. 108   *I am a man; nothing human is foreign to me*: Terence, *The Self-Tormentor*, Trans. Palmer Bovie (modified).

p. 109   *With humors dank and rank . . .*: Giuseppe Parini, "La salubrità dell'aria" (The Salubriousness of the Air).

p. 110   *Bigio*: the popular name of a Fascist-era marble colossus: a young, athletic man, meant to represent the ideals of the regime.

p. 112   *"But is it really possible not to doff your hat . . . ?"*: asked Pietro Mandré, Italian poet.

p. 114   *Zenga*: Walter.

p. 114   *O purity . . .*: a prayer of Jean-Pierre de Caussade (modified).

p. 116   *complement of circumscribed motion*, etc.: Italian grammatical terms for adverbial complements.

p. 116   *ornament and splendor of our age*: Ariosto, *Orlando Furioso*, I.3.

p. 117   *Diesseitig bin ich gar nicht fassbar*: "I cannot be grasped in the here and now." The beginning of a statement by Klee in a 1920 exhibition catalogue, which would later become his epitaph.

p. 119   *"the dark days are passed"*: Giosuè Carducci, "At the Sources of the Clitumnus," Trans. William Fletcher Smith.

p. 120   *patria est ubicumque est bene*: "One's country is wherever one is well," Cicero, *Tusculanae Disputationes*.

p. 120   *Lausberg*: Heinrich, German rhetorician.

p. 127   *Kranker im Boot*: Sick Man in a Boat.

p. 129   *Lepontian*: in reference to the ancient Celtic tribe of Switzerland, the Lepontii.

p. 131   *Italo Balbo*: Italo Balbo (1896–1940) was an Italian Black-shirt, Air Force Marshal, Governor-General of Libya, Commander-in-Chief of Italian North Africa, and "heir apparent" to Mussolini.

p. 131   *Tarascon at the death of Tartarin*: The city of Tarascon at the death of the hero Tartarin in Alphonse Daudet's adventure novel *Tartarin de Tarascon* (1872).

p. 138   *"à la guerre comme à la guerre!"*: French proverb, meaning "All's fair in war," or, "make the best of what you've got."

p. 140   *"like the blackbird with a little good weather"*: Purgatory XIII.123, Trans. W.S. Merwin.

p. 148   *the water-tower bird:* as in Klee's painting of the same name, 1937.

p. 148   *fetch Medusa, turn him into stone!*: Dante, *Inferno* IX.52, Trans. Ciaran Carson.

p. 150   *the great Francesco*: Francesco Guicciardini (1483–1540), author of the *Storia dell'Italia* (1537–40); Italian historian and statesman; one of the major Italian political writers of the Renaissance; a contemporary of Machiavelli's.

p. 150   *pinta trahit . . .*: "Pinta trahit pintam trahit altera pintula pintam et sic per pintas nascitur ebrietas." Medieval Latin drinking rhyme: "One pint leads to another, one little pint draws the next, and so pint by pint drunkenness is born."

p. 151   *as one great master of technique (de Caussade) says . . .*: Jean Pierre de Caussade, *Abandonment to Divine Providence*, Trans. Ignatius Strickland.

p. 153   *that actor was right*: i.e., Carmelo Bene.

p. 155   *Überschach*: Paul Klee, 1937.

p. 155   *Then he turned*: Dante, *Inferno* XV.121.

p. 157   *People are coming with whom I must not be*: Dante, *Inferno*, XV.118, Trans. Robert Durling.

p. 157   *and off he raced . . .*: Dante, *Inferno*, XV.121–124, Trans. Ciaran Carson (translation slightly modified).

GIOVANNI ORELLI (1928–) is a central figure in Swiss-Italian letters. He is the author of more than a dozen novels, as well as several books of poetry, and he has long been active in the cultural sphere of the Ticino. In 1997, he was awarded the Gottfried Keller Prize. *Walaschek's Dream* is his first novel to appear in English.

JAMIE RICHARDS is the translator of Nicolai Lilin's *Free Fall*, Serena Vitale's interviews with Viktor Shklovsky, *Witness to an Era*, and Giancarlo Pastore's *Jellyfish*, as well as short works by Ermanno Cavazzoni, Igort, and Giacomo Leopardi, among others.

PETROS ABATZOGLOU, *What Does Mrs. Freeman Want?*
MICHAL AJVAZ, *The Golden Age.*
The Other City.
PIERRE ALBERT-BIROT, *Grabinoulor.*
YUZ ALESHKOVSKY, *Kangaroo.*
FELIPE ALFAU, *Chromos.*
Locos.
JOÃO ALMINO, *The Book of Emotions.*
IVAN ÂNGELO, *The Celebration.*
The Tower of Glass.
DAVID ANTIN, *Talking.*
ANTÓNIO LOBO ANTUNES, *Knowledge of Hell.*
The Splendor of Portugal.
ALAIN ARIAS-MISSON, *Theatre of Incest.*
IFTIKHAR ARIF AND WAQAS KHWAJA, EDS.,
Modern Poetry of Pakistan.
JOHN ASHBERY AND JAMES SCHUYLER,
A Nest of Ninnies.
ROBERT ASHLEY, *Perfect Lives.*
GABRIELA AVIGUR-ROTEM, *Heatwave and Crazy Birds.*
HEIMRAD BÄCKER, *transcript.*
DJUNA BARNES, *Ladies Almanack.*
Ryder.
JOHN BARTH, *LETTERS.*
Sabbatical.
DONALD BARTHELME, *The King.*
Paradise.
SVETISLAV BASARA, *Chinese Letter.*
MIQUEL BAUÇÀ, *The Siege in the Room.*
RENÉ BELLETTO, *Dying.*
MAREK BIEŃCZYK, *Transparency.*
MARK BINELLI, *Sacco and Vanzetti Must Die!*
ANDREI BITOV, *Pushkin House.*
ANDREJ BLATNIK, *You Do Understand.*
LOUIS PAUL BOON, *Chapel Road.*
My Little War.
Summer in Termuren.
ROGER BOYLAN, *Killoyle.*
IGNÁCIO DE LOYOLA BRANDÃO,
Anonymous Celebrity.
The Good-Bye Angel.
Teeth under the Sun.
Zero.
BONNIE BREMSER, *Troia: Mexican Memoirs.*
CHRISTINE BROOKE-ROSE, *Amalgamemnon.*
BRIGID BROPHY, *In Transit.*
MEREDITH BROSNAN, *Mr. Dynamite.*
GERALD L. BRUNS, *Modern Poetry and the Idea of Language.*
EVGENY BUNIMOVICH AND J. KATES, EDS.,
Contemporary Russian Poetry: An Anthology.
GABRIELLE BURTON, *Heartbreak Hotel.*
MICHEL BUTOR, *Degrees.*
Mobile.
Portrait of the Artist as a Young Ape.
G. CABRERA INFANTE, *Infante's Inferno.*
Three Trapped Tigers.
JULIETA CAMPOS,
The Fear of Losing Eurydice.
ANNE CARSON, *Eros the Bittersweet.*
ORLY CASTEL-BLOOM, *Dolly City.*
CAMILO JOSÉ CELA, *Christ versus Arizona.*
The Family of Pascual Duarte.
The Hive.
LOUIS-FERDINAND CÉLINE, *Castle to Castle.*
Conversations with Professor Y.
London Bridge.

Normance.
North.
Rigadoon.
MARIE CHAIX, *The Laurels of Lake Constance.*
HUGO CHARTERIS, *The Tide Is Right.*
JEROME CHARYN, *The Tar Baby.*
ERIC CHEVILLARD, *Demolishing Nisard.*
LUIS CHITARRONI, *The No Variations.*
MARC CHOLODENKO, *Mordechai Schamz.*
JOSHUA COHEN, *Witz.*
EMILY HOLMES COLEMAN, *The Shutter of Snow.*
ROBERT COOVER, *A Night at the Movies.*
STANLEY CRAWFORD, *Log of the S.S. The Mrs Unguentine.*
Some Instructions to My Wife.
ROBERT CREELEY, *Collected Prose.*
RENÉ CREVEL, *Putting My Foot in It.*
RALPH CUSACK, *Cadenza.*
SUSAN DAITCH, *L.C.*
Storytown.
NICHOLAS DELBANCO, *The Count of Concord.*
Sherbrookes.
NIGEL DENNIS, *Cards of Identity.*
PETER DIMOCK, *A Short Rhetoric for Leaving the Family.*
ARIEL DORFMAN, *Konfidenz.*
COLEMAN DOWELL,
The Houses of Children.
Island People.
Too Much Flesh and Jabez.
ARKADII DRAGOMOSHCHENKO, *Dust.*
RIKKI DUCORNET, *The Complete Butcher's Tales.*
The Fountains of Neptune.
The Jade Cabinet.
The One Marvelous Thing.
Phosphor in Dreamland.
The Stain.
The Word "Desire."
WILLIAM EASTLAKE, *The Bamboo Bed.*
Castle Keep.
Lyric of the Circle Heart.
JEAN ECHENOZ, *Chopin's Move.*
STANLEY ELKIN, *A Bad Man.*
Boswell: A Modern Comedy.
Criers and Kibitzers, Kibitzers and Criers.
The Dick Gibson Show.
The Franchiser.
George Mills.
The Living End.
The MacGuffin.
The Magic Kingdom.
Mrs. Ted Bliss.
The Rabbi of Lud.
Van Gogh's Room at Arles.
FRANÇOIS EMMANUEL, *Invitation to a Voyage.*
ANNIE ERNAUX, *Cleaned Out.*
SALVADOR ESPRIU, *Ariadne in the Grotesque Labyrinth.*
LAUREN FAIRBANKS, *Muzzle Thyself.*
Sister Carrie.
LESLIE A. FIEDLER, *Love and Death in the American Novel.*
JUAN FILLOY, *Faction.*
Op Oloop.
ANDY FITCH, *Pop Poetics.*
GUSTAVE FLAUBERT, *Bouvard and Pécuchet.*
KASS FLEISHER, *Talking out of School.*

SELECTED DALKEY ARCHIVE TITLES

FORD MADOX FORD,
  The March of Literature.
JON FOSSE, *Aliss at the Fire.*
  Melancholy.
MAX FRISCH, *I'm Not Stiller.*
  Man in the Holocene.
CARLOS FUENTES, *Christopher Unborn.*
  Distant Relations.
  Terra Nostra.
  Vlad.
  Where the Air Is Clear.
TAKEHIKO FUKUNAGA, *Flowers of Grass.*
WILLIAM GADDIS, *J R.*
  The Recognitions.
JANICE GALLOWAY, *Foreign Parts.*
  The Trick Is to Keep Breathing.
WILLIAM H. GASS, *Cartesian Sonata
  and Other Novellas.*
  Finding a Form.
  A Temple of Texts.
  The Tunnel.
  Willie Masters' Lonesome Wife.
GÉRARD GAVARRY, *Hoppla! 1 2 3.*
  Making a Novel.
ETIENNE GILSON,
  The Arts of the Beautiful.
  Forms and Substances in the Arts.
C. S. GISCOMBE, *Giscome Road.*
  Here.
  Prairie Style.
DOUGLAS GLOVER, *Bad News of the Heart.*
  The Enamoured Knight.
WITOLD GOMBROWICZ,
  A Kind of Testament.
PAULO EMÍLIO SALES GOMES, *P's Three
  Women.*
KAREN ELIZABETH GORDON, *The Red Shoes.*
GEORGI GOSPODINOV, *Natural Novel.*
JUAN GOYTISOLO, *Count Julian.*
  Exiled from Almost Everywhere.
  Juan the Landless.
  Makbara.
  Marks of Identity.
PATRICK GRAINVILLE, *The Cave of Heaven.*
HENRY GREEN, *Back.*
  Blindness.
  Concluding.
  Doting.
  Nothing.
JACK GREEN, *Fire the Bastards!*
JIŘÍ GRUŠA, *The Questionnaire.*
GABRIEL GUDDING,
  Rhode Island Notebook.
MELA HARTWIG, *Am I a Redundant
  Human Being?*
JOHN HAWKES, *The Passion Artist.*
  Whistlejacket.
ELIZABETH HEIGHWAY, ED., *Contemporary
  Georgian Fiction.*
ALEKSANDAR HEMON, ED.,
  Best European Fiction.
AIDAN HIGGINS, *Balcony of Europe.*
  A Bestiary.
  Blind Man's Bluff
  Bornholm Night-Ferry.
  Darkling Plain: Texts for the Air.
  Flotsam and Jetsam.
  Langrishe, Go Down.
  Scenes from a Receding Past.
  Windy Arbours.
KEIZO HINO, *Isle of Dreams.*
KAZUSHI HOSAKA, *Plainsong.*

ALDOUS HUXLEY, *Antic Hay.*
  Crome Yellow.
  Point Counter Point.
  Those Barren Leaves.
  Time Must Have a Stop.
NAOYUKI II, *The Shadow of a Blue Cat.*
MIKHAIL IOSSEL AND JEFF PARKER, EDS.,
  *Amerika: Russian Writers View the
  United States.*
DRAGO JANČAR, *The Galley Slave.*
GERT JONKE, *The Distant Sound.*
  Geometric Regional Novel.
  Homage to Czerny.
  The System of Vienna.
JACQUES JOUET, *Mountain R.*
  Savage.
  Upstaged.
CHARLES JULIET, *Conversations with
  Samuel Beckett and Bram van
  Velde.*
MIEKO KANAI, *The Word Book.*
YORAM KANIUK, *Life on Sandpaper.*
HUGH KENNER, *The Counterfeiters.*
  *Flaubert, Joyce and Beckett:
  The Stoic Comedians.*
  Joyce's Voices.
DANILO KIŠ, *The Attic.*
  Garden, Ashes.
  The Lute and the Scars
  Psalm 44.
  A Tomb for Boris Davidovich.
ANITA KONKKA, *A Fool's Paradise.*
GEORGE KONRÁD, *The City Builder.*
TADEUSZ KONWICKI, *A Minor Apocalypse.*
  The Polish Complex.
MENIS KOUMANDAREAS, *Koula.*
ELAINE KRAF, *The Princess of 72nd Street.*
JIM KRUSOE, *Iceland.*
AYŞE KULIN, *Farewell: A Mansion in
  Occupied Istanbul.*
EWA KURYLUK, *Century 21.*
EMILIO LASCANO TEGUI, *On Elegance
  While Sleeping.*
ERIC LAURRENT, *Do Not Touch.*
HERVÉ LE TELLIER, *The Sextine Chapel.*
  *A Thousand Pearls (for a Thousand
  Pennies)*
VIOLETTE LEDUC, *La Bâtarde.*
EDOUARD LEVÉ, *Autoportrait.*
  Suicide.
MARIO LEVI, *Istanbul Was a Fairy Tale.*
SUZANNE JILL LEVINE, *The Subversive
  Scribe: Translating Latin
  American Fiction.*
DEBORAH LEVY, *Billy and Girl.*
  *Pillow Talk in Europe and Other
  Places.*
JOSÉ LEZAMA LIMA, *Paradiso.*
ROSA LIKSOM, *Dark Paradise.*
OSMAN LINS, *Avalovara.*
  The Queen of the Prisons of Greece.
ALF MAC LOCHLAINN,
  The Corpus in the Library.
  Out of Focus.
RON LOEWINSOHN, *Magnetic Field(s).*
MINA LOY, *Stories and Essays of Mina Loy.*
BRIAN LYNCH, *The Winner of Sorrow.*
D. KEITH MANO, *Take Five.*
MICHELINE AHARONIAN MARCOM,
  The Mirror in the Well.
BEN MARCUS,
  The Age of Wire and String.

FOR A FULL LIST OF PUBLICATIONS, VISIT:
www.dalkeyarchive.com

SELECTED DALKEY ARCHIVE TITLES

The Princess Hoppy.
Some Thing Black.
LEON S. ROUDIEZ, *French Fiction Revisited.*
RAYMOND ROUSSEL, *Impressions of Africa.*
VEDRANA RUDAN, *Night.*
STIG SÆTERBAKKEN, *Siamese.*
LYDIE SALVAYRE, *The Company of Ghosts.*
Everyday Life.
The Lecture.
Portrait of the Writer as a
Domesticated Animal.
The Power of Flies.
LUIS RAFAEL SÁNCHEZ,
Macho Camacho's Beat.
SEVERO SARDUY, *Cobra & Maitreya.*
NATHALIE SARRAUTE,
Do You Hear Them?
Martereau.
The Planetarium.
ARNO SCHMIDT, *Collected Novellas.*
Collected Stories.
Nobodaddy's Children.
Two Novels.
ASAF SCHURR, *Motti.*
CHRISTINE SCHUTT, *Nightwork.*
GAIL SCOTT, *My Paris.*
DAMION SEARLS, *What We Were Doing*
and Where We Were Going.
JUNE AKERS SEESE,
Is This What Other Women Feel Too?
What Waiting Really Means.
BERNARD SHARE, *Inish.*
Transit.
AURELIE SHEEHAN, *Jack Kerouac Is Pregnant.*
VIKTOR SHKLOVSKY, *Bowstring.*
Knight's Move.
A Sentimental Journey:
Memoirs 1917–1922.
Energy of Delusion: A Book on Plot.
Literature and Cinematography.
Theory of Prose.
Third Factory.
Zoo, or Letters Not about Love.
CLAUDE SIMON, *The Invitation.*
PIERRE SINIAC, *The Collaborators.*
KJERSTI A. SKOMSVOLD, *The Faster I Walk,*
the Smaller I Am.
JOSEF ŠKVORECKÝ, *The Engineer of*
Human Souls.
GILBERT SORRENTINO,
Aberration of Starlight.
Blue Pastoral.
Crystal Vision.
Imaginative Qualities of Actual
Things.
Mulligan Stew.
Pack of Lies.
Red the Fiend.
The Sky Changes.
Something Said.
Splendide-Hôtel.
Steelwork.
Under the Shadow.
W. M. SPACKMAN, *The Complete Fiction.*
ANDRZEJ STASIUK, *Dukla.*
Fado.
GERTRUDE STEIN, *Lucy Church Amiably.*
The Making of Americans.
A Novel of Thank You.
LARS SVENDSEN, *A Philosophy of Evil.*
PIOTR SZEWC, *Annihilation.*
GONÇALO M. TAVARES, *Jerusalem.*

Joseph Walser's Machine.
Learning to Pray in the Age of
Technique.
LUCIAN DAN TEODOROVICI,
Our Circus Presents . . .
NIKANOR TERATOLOGEN, *Assisted Living.*
STEFAN THEMERSON, *Hobson's Island.*
The Mystery of the Sardine.
Tom Harris.
TAEKO TOMIOKA, *Building Waves.*
JOHN TOOMEY, *Sleepwalker.*
JEAN-PHILIPPE TOUSSAINT, *The Bathroom.*
Camera.
Monsieur.
Reticence.
Running Away.
Self-Portrait Abroad.
Television.
The Truth about Marie.
DUMITRU TSEPENEAG, *Hotel Europa.*
The Necessary Marriage.
Pigeon Post.
Vain Art of the Fugue.
ESTHER TUSQUETS, *Stranded.*
DUBRAVKA UGRESIC, *Lend Me Your Character.*
Thank You for Not Reading.
TOR ULVEN, *Replacement.*
MATI UNT, *Brecht at Night.*
Diary of a Blood Donor.
Things in the Night.
ÁLVARO URIBE AND OLIVIA SEARS, EDS.,
Best of Contemporary Mexican Fiction.
ELOY URROZ, *Friction.*
The Obstacles.
LUISA VALENZUELA, *Dark Desires and*
the Others.
He Who Searches.
MARJA-LIISA VARTIO, *The Parson's Widow.*
PAUL VERHAEGHEN, *Omega Minor.*
AGLAJA VETERANYI, *Why the Child Is*
Cooking in the Polenta.
BORIS VIAN, *Heartsnatcher.*
LLORENÇ VILLALONGA, *The Dolls' Room.*
TOOMAS VINT, *An Unending Landscape.*
ORNELA VORPSI, *The Country Where No*
One Ever Dies.
AUSTRYN WAINHOUSE, *Hedyphagetica.*
PAUL WEST, *Words for a Deaf Daughter*
& Gala.
CURTIS WHITE, *America's Magic Mountain.*
The Idea of Home.
Memories of My Father Watching TV.
Monstrous Possibility: An Invitation
to Literary Politics.
Requiem.
DIANE WILLIAMS, *Excitability:*
Selected Stories.
Romancer Erector.
DOUGLAS WOOLF, *Wall to Wall.*
Ya! & John-Juan.
JAY WRIGHT, *Polynomials and Pollen.*
The Presentable Art of Reading
Absence.
PHILIP WYLIE, *Generation of Vipers.*
MARGUERITE YOUNG, *Angel in the Forest.*
Miss MacIntosh, My Darling.
REYOUNG, *Unbabbling.*
VLADO ŽABOT, *The Succubus.*
ZORAN ŽIVKOVIĆ, *Hidden Camera.*
LOUIS ZUKOFSKY, *Collected Fiction.*
VITOMIL ZUPAN, *Minuet for Guitar.*
SCOTT ZWIREN, *God Head.*